VOICE
FROM THE

A ghost story of Robin Hood's Bay

JOHN GILMAN

First published 1998 by Marine Arts Publications (Deckchair Books)
"Seascape"
Robin Hood's Bay,
Whitby, North Yorkshire,
England. YO22 4SH.

ISBN 0-9516184-7-4
Voices from the Sea.

Front cover painting © by
Caroline Bebington.

Line drawings © by
John Gilman.

Printed by Crewe Colour Printers Limited
Crewe Road, Wheelock,
Sandbach,Cheshire,
CW11 4YS

DEDICATION

To Andrew Talbot, Mariner,
1531-1607
his only memorial,
and
Sara, who has no known grave.

ACKNOWLEDGEMENTS

My sincere thanks to both residents and long term visitors to Robin Hood's Bay for their permission to record two of the fascinating ghost stories that are to be found here. Obviously some of the locations and names have had to be changed otherwise these stories would never have found their way into print. There is, however, sufficient evidence to verify these experiences as many folk will attest. During the last thirty years I have discovered many more stories that warrant research but we shall have to wait awhile before they command the resources they deserve. Should you encounter a ghost in these narrow streets, don't flinch, they have a story to tell and they seek our compassion and understanding.

Each of my drawings has a psychic significance, mostly from the pages of this book but I am sure you will discover other significant settings for yourselves as you explore this unique and magical township.

'There are verily and indeed Spirits and Phantoms which sometimes appear to men, and not unseldom we are confronted with marvellous and most unexpected supernatural occurrences.'

Father Noel Taillepied, 1540-1589,
Priest and Scholar of the Capuchin Order.

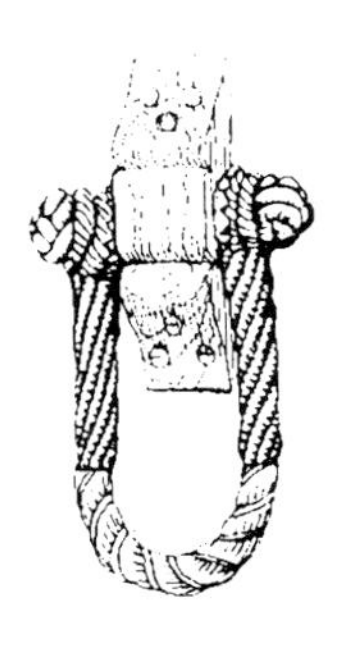

CHAPTER ONE

Shortly after midnight the wind freshened and worked up to a gale. With each successive gust the dull brass lantern under the cottage porch swung drunkenly on its short chain and drummed against the scarred wooden lintel. Only yards below a great black sea surged and slopped over the roadway below the Bay Hotel leaving pebbles and tangled skeins of bladderwrack strewn across the narrow Dock and the base of New Road.

It wasn't the lantern that woke him. It was that other noise again. At first during the summers when he'd started to come regularly to this little cottage for a well earned annual rest he'd not noticed it. It was only when he'd finally retired and became accustomed to the regular creaks and groans of the old building that he'd reluctantly arrived at the conclusion that there was something else within the walls of the cottage. Of course he didn't accept the idea easily. The last thing that he wanted to admit was the possibility of a ghost. He'd never really given the subject much thought. However, after carefully eliminating all the identified sounds, he was always left with this very human noise as if someone was singing or humming an old repetitive tune just under their breath. Once, slightly amused at his reaction, he'd tracked the sound down during one Autumn gale and discovered that it was more evident close to the old pockmarked yellow limestone mantel in the front parlour where, if he cared to admit it, he had the strangest feeling that he was not alone. There, by the open fire, on more than one occasion he thought he could hear the regular rhythm of breathing close at hand. Not the breathing of a youngster but the chesty exhalation of an older man. Once he distinctly heard him clear his throat. Then when the gales subsided the noises ceased and the room became his own again.

Tonight, now wide awake, he'd heard the singing again, a deep regular melody, repeated over and over and just audible above a wind that bullied and a tide that spilled up and sucked hungrily back across the smooth cobbles at the base of the Dock slip. He took the poker and scratched the dying fire into a poor flame and put a log on the back. He then drew up his favourite chair to the brightening grate and stretched out with a wry smile. Around him the shadows jerked and flickered as if in tune with the elemental orchestra out there in the Bay beyond the reach of the most intrepid mariner.

Commander Richard Jordan-Squires had long returned from the sea and not so long retired from a senior position with a prominent national paper manufacturer. He'd promised himself a berth by the seaside when his working life was over and this summer cottage in Robin Hood's Bay was the answer to all his prayers.

He and his wife Sylvia had discovered Bay in 1947 when on his final leave from the Royal Navy. It had been his first real holiday since 1939 when his life, in common with thousands of others, had been turned upside down.

Driving off the moor on his way from Scarborough to Whitby he'd been intrigued by the name and then amazed at what he'd found at the bottom of the hill. As today, Bay exuded that timeless quality that transcends the now and allows the visitor to stand where he will in the scheme of things. Like many Cornish and Devon fishing villages, Bay had been an insular working township, a place of boats, nets and hard work, but as the fisher families declined and the practicalities and economics of the industry moved to Whitby, Bay was left to dream, untouched by post-war development, the iconoclasm of the sixties and the concrete flamboyance of the eighties. Bay survived, having the ingredients of a modest success as a holiday centre with its hundreds of small cottages, its seafaring and smuggling heritage, its history and folklore and its unique position, tumbling down the cliff to an invincible sea.

Dick had fallen in love with the place on first sight. There were several cottages to let and one in particular, just up from the Dock, half way up King Street, seemed to fit the bill. The Dolphin Inn was almost next door, the beach only yards away and from his step he could relish the sight and scent of the sea, a refreshing reminder of the better times during the war and a long way from the city where, inevitably, he must suffer the clamour and din of the commercial fray. Instinctively he felt a bolt-hole like this would provide just the right antidote to counter the growing stress of the business years that lay ahead. Sylvia thought the place charming, the few folk that she had met warm and genuinely welcoming and so, rather than press on up the coast for further holiday accommodation, they decided to rent for the rest of the fortnight and explore this bewitching little township.

That first summer in Bay set the seal on the dozens of years that followed and when the children came along the beaches, cliffs and scaurs proved to be a great favourite with the girls and they quickly learned their way around the maze of tiny streets, entries, yards and steps. Dick tried several cottages over the years, in Tommy Baxter Street, Chapel Street and Fisherhead but always seemed to feel particularly at home in the King Street cottage so when, in 1967, it came up for sale he bought it and visited as often as his life allowed. He never felt inclined to let it but as the children grew older it was seldom empty and family and friends soon made it their base for a traditional English summer holiday. Dick always valued the fact that Bay somehow preserved the magic of his own childhood with so many traditional elements unspoiled. He loved the beach, the bright streams, the changing moods, and the subtle varieties of colour in the beachscape, now a scrambled profusion of insistent green and now part of a grey, crawling, prowling ocean. He found a timeless quality here where the trappings of fashion and progress had somehow passed by and left Bay much as it had been for generations. It had certainly not changed since he first found it and no-one was in a hurry to import the neon arcades and the shrill pain of insistent greed. Life was different here and he could sense it as he descended the steep bank away from the roads and connections with the rest of the world. The shops that sold to children and tourists were there, true enough, but they did not dominate, whilst the pubs, restaurants, tea-rooms, book shops, exhibitions and a small sensitively arranged museum added to the qualities still sought by a growing number of more discerning holiday-makers. He quickly discovered that there were other families who enjoyed long-term love affairs with Bay and in high summer and at Christmas time they met up again and again watching each others' children grow up until they, in their growing sophistication, decided they had outgrown it, only to return a few years later with children of their own. It was truly a place apart and probably unique on the coasts of England.

He shifted a little in his fireside chair. The log had almost gone and the room grew smaller. Outside, the wind pushed aggressively against the dark stones and he was glad not to be out in the thick of it as he had been on so many unavoidable occasions. Within the walls, the deep sonorous theme seemed to rise and fall with the gale. It was a simple melody that invited repetition and probably carried many verses. It also carried a rhythmic pattern that seemed somehow familiar although he couldn't quite place it. On this occasion he thought he could pick out a few words here and there. Funny thing, but he no longer felt alarmed, puzzled or curious about his visitor. Rather he accepted him as a part of the house and had to admit that if he somehow stopped he'd miss this peculiarity of the place.

He'd asked a few discreet questions at first and soon discovered that there were other strange stories about Bay. Some had been investigated and some hadn't. Some had found their way into local history and legend and some, of course, were bound up with the activities of the smuggling fraternity who were particularly keen to promote a self-imposed curfew for fear of the supernatural. Nevertheless, there were several stories that persisted with credible experience to back them up. In this particular case, he'd decided to let sleeping dogs lie and not push further than to investigate the age of his cottage, the land on which it was built and the history of the street.

The cottage, he discovered, was older that the date which had been painted over the door which was the date of the earliest parchment deed transferring the property to James Henry Fewster, fisher. The previous owner, one Tarbet or Talbot had died without heir or will and was only known by virtue of his mark on a petition preserved at the museum library in Whitby in which a plea for parochial support had been launched in the December of 1597 for the assistance of the fisher folk living in King Henry Street, Robin Hood's Bay, whose dwellings had been extensively damaged by a severe storm that engulfed the seaward hillside. It was signed by name and by mark by those inhabitants of King Henry Street that were leaseholders, householders, mariners or fishermen. That Tarbet was a mariner was evidenced by his mark, an anchor with the stock extended to form an initial.

During routine repairs to the cottage Dick discovered that much of the old timber panelling was worm-eaten and rotten and upon ripping out the panelling in the front parlour found that the front elevation had been rebuilt in stone at some time. The lower courses, the chimney breast and sections of the party walls were of a different size of stone, bigger than the rest and having very little mortar between the blocks, revealing, so he had been told by a local builder, that the cottage had been rebuilt somewhere early in the seventeenth century. Once the plaster was off the old chimney breast several interesting old initials were discovered carved into the stones. There were no prominent letter T's unless a crudely carved anchor bore a longer stock than was common and might be interpreted as a T. It was too far gone to be certain.

The road was easier. Apparently there was documentary evidence to support that the street was named from a group of tenements held by the crown 'tempus Henry V11I' and that these had passed to his daughter Elizabeth on her accession to the throne. She, however, being always strapped for cash and always under pressure to support her kingdom as a growing European power, sold the properties locally in 1536. That same year the travelling topographer Leland described Bay as a thriving fishing village with a significant fleet of local craft which would necessitate a wide range of supportive industries and skills. So King Street existed, likely as the main road to the Dock, and along the winding descending roadway would have been the buildings to support the fleet, sail lofts, ropewalks, blockworks and the like. Bordering the crowded access to the beach would have been slips, shipwright's sheds and the smoking houses for preserving the catch. It would have been an almost self-sufficient community with the bulk of necessary transport coming in by sea.

The sixteenth century saw a break in the continuity of a stable monastic influence and many of the old patterns of trade were severed. Certainly in this region, the demise of the Abbey at Whitby meant that the town's jetty came under local control for the first time in centuries. The transport of animals, hides, tallow, salt, timber and stone that had been under Abbey administration now fell to local initiative and each boat owner and local leaseholder found it a struggle to set up fresh patterns of trade and adjust to their new landlords. Even the foreshore fishing rights had belonged to the Abbey but under the new laws they had reverted to the Crown and it was to be some time before the new leases were brought into effect. Independent fisher townships with their own fleets like Bay and Staithes fared better than older Whitby where the fishing industry had served not only the Abbey and the local community but the Abbey's connections throughout the north.

He became aware of the ticking of the clock and noticed that it was after one in the morning. He'd been dozing. Outside the wind had moderated and the tide had started to withdraw. Pale curtains of salt sleet spray were still hosing right over the Bay Hotel and opposite the cottage the repeated thuds of the waves hitting the sea wall told him that it would be an hour or two before this storm pressed tide would retreat down the beach once more. He sighed and shifted in his chair, allowing his eyes to wander about the familiar furniture and favourite pictures of their retirement home. Some things had been friends for over forty years, he mused. There wasn't much really. It was amazing how their needs were satisfied with little. He remembered that some Greek philosopher or other had said that true happiness did not lie in possessions but in that which one could, with dignity, do without. That was certainly true. Now that they were retired, they were perfectly happy with the basics and didn't feel the urge to gain anything more.

Yes. He and Sylvia loved it here. Here was peace. Here he could experience the passage of the seasons and a gentler pace of life that need not plan further than the week ahead. No pressures and no worries and the time to listen to the stories of their children's passage through the ocean of life and hopefully being able to help them now and again in as many ways as they could.

A loud cough, right opposite him brought a surprised smile and for a brief moment he could have sworn he saw a figure grinning back at him from the other side of the fireplace. He must have fallen asleep.

Sylvia slept through the gale. By six o'clock an inquisitive morning sun had probed the storm-scrubbed scaurs and glistened on the patches of newly turned sand. The few ragged clouds soon shifted to the north east leaving a fresh wind to dry out the sandy streets. On descending the steep stairway, she noticed Dick still sound asleep in his chair and realised he'd been up in the night. She went through into the kitchen and soon the smell of coffee filtered back into the parlour. With a grunt, Dick heaved himself upright, and yawned. He'd slept well despite being awoken by the storm. He rose and went across to the salted window. Then he glanced back towards the grate. Silly dream. The cottage seemed strangely still after the roaring night.

They shared coffee and toast whilst listening to the familiar pattern of Radio Four. Sylvia's routine was much the same each weekday morning. She helped to run a small book shop in Bay. Situated just off the Bank, it gave her an outlet for her passion for words and reading as well as allowing her the opportunity to join in the pleasant daily interaction as folk left their vehicles at the top of the village and wandered, willy-nilly, down among the jumbled collection of history and legend apparent before them.

Whilst Dick had been in the Royal Navy during the war, Sylvia had nursed, including nursing in London right through the Blitz. They both had sharp memories of the war. They had married in 1942 when times were as mercurial as they could have been so their union was one tested early in the crucible of war which enabled them to stand strong when the uncertain sands of business shifted them more than once from their home.

Sylvia's insight into life was literally forged in fire and she had developed a deep inner strength that had resonated down through the years. She knew her early training had paid off in the self-knowledge and discipline that brought her the courage others envied. They'd made a good couple from the start. He, a tall, fine-looking man, who carried his ability to lead with authority and experience; she, attractive, practical and enthusiastic with an endless energy that enabled her to become involved in community life where she was greatly appreciated. Both had a horror of idleness and though Dick had deliberately slowed down, he still found time to help whenever called upon. Sylvia however, shuffled the many tasks of the day like a card-sharp spreading a multitude of tasks throughout the hours with a practiced economy of effort. Her advice was worth listening to.

Their two daughters kept in close touch. Pam, now living in New Zealand, had settled after an adventurous life which had taken her all over the world. She returned to the U.K. as often as she could and loved indulging herself in Bay with all the attendant nostalgia of a happy childhood spent on the foreshore and on the moors above. She loved the sturdy Georgian and Queen Anne vernacular architecture and could still take a visitor to a particular cottage or high house to look at a window or doorway. Her visits with her New Zealand born husband and her grown-up son were always looked forward to with great anticipation and hugely enjoyed.

Annie was the quiet one, thoughtful and deep thinking. She had suffered a disastrous marriage which had left her with the responsibility of bringing up two teenage sons without any support. Always the sensitive, generous and giving soul, she had given her all to a man who'd proved irresponsible and unappreciative. Before very long he had vanished with another partner and left Annie without a home and without the involvement that her growing sons needed from a father. He saw them occasionally, but only enough to disorientate them and upset the balance and order that Annie tried to bring into their lives. Her trips to Bay had a two-fold purpose, to draw strength from her mother and to find afresh the delights of the place where she'd enjoyed so many happy memories as a child.

On some occasions, when they all found themselves in Bay at the same time, the wine and conversation flowed, the contemporary scene vanished, and they were just a family in which love and memories strengthened their bonds by the minute.

Like her husband, ever since their arrival in Bay, Sylvia had been interested in the history of the town. Alongside the history however, there was a wealth of folk-lore which fascinated her. Apart from the smuggling stories which were rich enough, preserving something of the days when the whole town was engaged in a private war to overcome the stiff duties payable on certain recognised necessities, there were the ghost stories that cropped up with a puzzling regularity. Only when she'd heard the same story told by two different people about their experience in a particular cottage did she conclude that something or someone was living out a drama that extended across decades.

Of course every old town has its ghosts simply because every town has seen its share of human drama and tragedy that has left its patterns and marks down the years. In turn, gale, wreck and death had made their inroads into the psychic fabric of the old town and there were dozens of stories that warranted investigation, if only to lay troubled spirits to rest or to separate the very real human dramas from the urban myths and the always popular fabrications enjoyed by the visitors.

A regularly recurring story concerned a cottage at the top of King Street. They'd both heard it during their first visit in 1947 and it seemed to surface every year or so as various visitors experienced it. The last time was late in the eighties and as far as Sylvia could ascertain, it had not happened in the nineties, or at least, she had not heard it talked about in the book shop.

Apparently a schoolmistress on holiday from Staffordshire had taken a cottage at the top of King Street in the summer of 1988. She had felt particularly rested after a hectic term and had managed to extend her holiday from two weeks to three due to a cancellation. During the third week, on the Thursday, she awakened to find a still, brilliantly moonlit night flooding through her dormer window. Without really questioning why, she rose and looked out across a silver splashed sea beyond dark patterns of roofs and chimneys. The peace, after the persistent clamour of children, shrill gulls and the boisterous late-night comradeship of the Dolphin seemed unassailable.

From a distance, she heard the sound of a hard-pressed galloping horse. Being a horse owner herself, she was immediately concerned that someone should be riding so furiously in steep streets in the dark and she feared for the animal's safety. She was soon even more alarmed as, minutes later, the horse was heard to arrive blowing and snorting in a flurry of scattered stones directly below her window followed by a thunderous knocking on the front door. Fumbling with the window catch she pushed up the sash and peered out. She had a clear view of the street below and the front of the house. No horse and no rider. As she watched and listened, she heard boots on gravel and the squeak of leather as the rider re-mounted. Then she heard the horse respond and break into a canter up the street towards the bank top.

Mystified, and wondering if someone was experiencing some kind of emergency, she worried again about the horse. There was nothing else to do but go back to bed which she did. In the morning she sensibly went over the events of the night but, finding no gravel outside and no road beyond the cottage up which to canter, she felt forced to admit to a psychic experience of some kind.

Sylvia found this account more lucidly presented than the stories from the fifties and sixties, but they all amounted to the same thing. There was more than one independent witness to some forgotten drama from the past.

The story Richard found fascinating but inexplicable was the one that his friend and brother officer had confided to him after his first visit in 1958. Sitting in the Dolphin one June night Bill, who had been First Lieutenant of the corvette *Myosotis,* had left about 2245 to find his way back to a cottage he was renting in Tommy Baxter Street. He'd had a few pints but nothing that would impede his unaccompanied journey a few hundreds yards up the town. He'd turned left into Chapel Street and right through the Openings. It was a bright, clear night and an indigo sky revealed a waning moon low over Ravenscar. When among the cottages beyond the Openings he'd somehow missed his way and fell in with a local character who'd also had a jar or two. Together the pair laughed and meandered their way up the hill until his new companion stopped and said,

'Shhh! I go in here. God be with ee.'

He opened a door, grinned, and quietly went in. Bill, realising he'd gone further than he needed, turned back and quickly found the Square and then walked on down to Tommy Baxter Street.

He particularly remembered the house where his new friend had lived because it was under a dark, overhanging section of building and the door was on the left down a yard. All efforts to find it again proved negative and the nearest he remembered took him along Cliff Street into an area long fallen over the cliff.

Working in the book shop gave Sylvia the opportunity to talk to a lot of visitors as well as the local inhabitants, including her workmate who had some amazing stories of her own. These included the current, ongoing stories that surfaced regularly every year as more and more people saw and heard things that were beyond normal experience. There was the little waif that was seen begging at the end of Chapel Street and outside the old bakery. Clad only in a dirty shift, she posed a pathetic figure as she wandered the street between The Laurel and the Openings. More persistent were the experiences recorded in a cottage off the Bank where another girl from the past regularly provided spectacular and mischievious effects usually for visitors and workmen. All of the inns in the town had their stories too. However, it wasn't only the town that had its ghosts, the beach had its fair share.

THE
BAY
HOTEL
COCOA
1998

CHAPTER TWO

The familiar moon had followed Sara like a welcome coin until, exhausted, she halted her lonely flight high on the bare moor. She noticed that she was not far from her intended destination. Far below her, under the collected shadows of the hill, a soundless sea flashed and glinted in the uncertain night. Way, way out, anonymous shipping crawled up the coast, too slow it seemed to get anywhere. Only as her breathing gradually subsided did she acknowledge that the storm was hers and that the night beyond the car's wild beams was still. She leaned forward and switched off the shuddering engine and eased, still trembling, from the driving seat. The air was chill.

The moon, which had been slipping silently through a shallow night of broken cloud had come to rest above Ravenscar. She leaned back hard against the cold metal, still endeavouring to control her breathing. She made a deliberate attempt to relax the muscles of her face, shoulders and neck but was only partly successful. As her breathing became a little more manageable, she traced the end of her journey down among the switchbacked, black, bush-carpeted tumbled hillside towards her goal still hidden by the bulk of the bending moor's plunge into the sea.

Robin Hood's Bay, where she'd come so often as a child and less often than she'd wanted as an adult. For her Bay was a place of refuge, a retreat, an out of the way place where she'd learned to lose herself and the problems that had always seemed to assault her. How well she knew those problems. She had been twice cursed, though both curses had always been seen enviously by others as blessings. At first when Sara realised that she had been born with looks that others envied, she'd been pleased but when she became the victim of bullying, hatred and abuse, she fled puzzled, first into truancy and then into the sanctuary of solitude where the second curse soon manifested itself. She discovered by the age of seven that she was acutely sensitive to a vast range of experiences so that her depression was as sharp as her delight. Thus equippped for life, she skimmed like a stone across troubled water, now soaring but inevitably plunging into the darker unswimable reaches below.

Her first confrontation with the world had been in school when she was eight. The war was reaching its climax with the landings in Normandy and a steady Allied advance towards the Rhine. She'd been allocated to a new teacher that September and was looking forward to the start of a fresh class. Her old teacher, Miss Shaddock had been a kindly, encouraging spinster already past retirement age who had looked benignly upon her charges as very much her own children. They had all loved her. The new teacher was far from benign. Obviously wishing to avoid any battles with her potential enemy she decided attack was the best weapon she could muster. She would have no nonsense. From the first moment her energies were exercised not in what she could give to the class but what she would do to it. Thus, from the first hour of the first morning no-one was left in any doubt about where they stood. The battle lines were drawn and the initial casualties were among the weaker, hesitant boys whose penmanship left a trail that would have puzzled a Gestalt psychologist with no part contributing to the whole and by no means all of it on the page. Some she caned with a delight that was uncomfortable to watch. Others she pinched, tweaked and poked with a tight-mouthed intent. After one terrible afternoon in which she abandoned teaching for invective, the dazed victims returned erratically to their seats guided by the outstretched hands of their friends. Life in the class was becoming impossible.

Of course Sara told her parents but they felt sure she was exaggerating. The Headteacher was alerted by more than one parent and the Governors were telephoned but whenever the Head left his office and looked into Miss Hillem's classroom he saw only rows of quiet children paying assiduous attention. The class was a model of good behaviour.

Sara was a bright child and soon recognised the value of keeping her head down to avoid the shrapnel. However her turn came one morning when the class was brought to attention whilst Miss Hillem attempted to drum in the dates of the Civil War. Miss was beginning to enjoy power and one of the ways in which she could demonstrate this was to single out a particular child in front of a quietened class and reduce it to tears. On this occasion her gaze trained around the class like an anti-aircraft gunner, past the battle-weary ranks of boys and came to rest on Sara sitting upright in her desk and facing forward. She was quite startlingly pretty and Miss Hillem's eyes half closed.

Angela, sitting behind Sara, muttered,

'Oh-oh, Sara, Himmler's got her sights on you.'

'You girl,' roared Himmler. 'What did you call me?'

'Nothing Miss,' whispered Sara, genuinely fearful and innocent.

'Do you think I'm a fool girl?' she screamed. 'Do you think I'm bloody deaf?'

'No Miss.'

'No Miss what?'

'No Miss Hillem.'

'How dare you speak to me like that you ill-mannered child! Stand up.'

Sara stood up slowly, the eyes of the whole class emphasising her vulnerability. She paled and held herself still, her fingers pressed against the bottom of the desk lid.

'Stand up straight.'

It was when Sara's eyes rose to meet the narrowed glare focussed upon her that the full impact of this confrontation became obvious to the whole class but so much more obvious to Miss Hillem. Here was innocent, sensitive beauty met with thwarted bitterness and unresolved frustration. Never would Miss Hillem approach the potential of her pupil in any direction and instinctively, she knew it. Only now, in this situation, could she do anything about it and so she fell into the trap that is the temptation of so many teachers and used the only opportunity that she would ever have to hit out at fate.

Miss Hillem walked slowly to a position just behind Sara. Then, talking softly, she took her apart with a triumphant bitterness whilst stabbing her again and again in the back with her forefinger. Inevitably, as Sara knew it must, the climax came with a full swing from behind, high on Sara's cheek which sent her staggering, blind, into the aisle between the desks.

'Don't you ever think that because you are a pretty pretty you can get away with it. Now, get out! Get out!'

This was the first time that Sara had come to realise that there were situations in which she was powerless and entirely out of her depth. It was not going to be the last.

She'd left the car now and had started on down the rough hillside. As she re-lived those days of fourteen years ago she'd come off the track and plunged into heather, ling and low scrub. The moon had lowered and there was a distinct orange pre-dawn glow in the eastern sky. She reckoned it must be well after four, perhaps even five o' clock and the night was almost over. Determined to watch the sun rise up out of the sea from the water's edge she pushed on, past dark rocky outcrops and dense gorse until, quite by accident, she found the track again as it turned northwards under the steepest part of the hill.

She'd first watched the sunrise during the holiday she was twelve. She'd had the uppermost room in a cottage on the seaward side of King Street and the dormer window looked out over the sea. She'd propped herself up in bed opposite the window and watched as the unfamiliar daily drama unfolded before her. She was enthralled as yellows and bright golds folded over pinks and purples to colour miles of wrinkled ocean and sky. It changed every minute until the shy disc of the sun pulled itself out of the sea and flexed into an unstarable, unbelievable brilliance and the sky above lightened into a vibrant blue flecked with puffs of silver embroidered icing. It was so delightful, she'd recorded it in her holiday diary.

Her other great discovery was the beach where she went more eagerly each day. Whether on the scaurs or walking out towards Ravenscar, she loved every minute of the changing day from the wave mist obscuring the far cliff profile to the myriad glistening sea-washed fragments as they tumbled over and over in the wake of the sea's pull down the beach. Once she'd cried as she'd heard Pachelbel's Canon being played on the wireless above her head in Beacholme as she sat looking at the Bay before the summer crowds had invaded the beach. It was just perfect and she knew somehow that it would never change. On more than a few bright, gleaming sun-washed days she'd found her favourite place up a little used path beyond Stoup Beck to the cliff top overlooking the beach where she'd sit hugging her knees and staring into the high cloudscape that crept silently above the roofs of Robin Hood's Bay.

Then she fell, and the jolt brought her back to the present. Pain swamped her for those first few intense moments then flowed back into her body leaving her bleeding freely from both knees. Her ankle was badly sprained and she only managed to struggle up with difficulty. She looked down at herself. Her long skirt was torn and her blouse snagged. She was a mess. Her life was a mess. One thought remained. She would go on down to the beach. So, pulling herself together, she limped on down the lane towards the beach leaving tiny drops of bright blood in little starlike splashes on the rough tarmac. They were like the landmarks of disappointment in her life, each one a building block in the teetering, unstable tenement where her soul had uncertain lodging. The islands of peace had been few and it was always her return to Robin Hood's Bay that had brought her a measure of happiness and an escape from the world.

Above the eastern horizon, a new day was stretching into the sky which was still dark above the pale westering moon. Ravenscar's dark bulk threatened behind her and under the curved claws of sharp rock the sea chuckled in the pre-dawn quiet. As a light dew quickly formed, a low, hardly visible mist floated wraithlike just above the dip behind the cliff-tops. A single crow's plaintive falling note sounded out from the trees at the laneside and she stopped to gather her strength. There was no way down here. The cliffs, though not high, were too steep. It needed a further few minutes down the track to the rough stone-clad pathway to the beach. Her last few yards were difficult and just before the end she wandered off to the right and found a sheltered spot among the tangled undergrowth at the edge of the field. She'd wait for sufficient light to see her way. She sat, hunched up with her back to the sea, her arms clasping her knees in much the same pose as she'd adopted on a hundred sunnier mornings long ago. As it slowly became lighter, a thin breeze ruffled across the surface of the sea leaving irregular ribbons of broken water in a haphazard pattern of disturbed light and she became aware for the first time of the sound of gentle waves licking at the sand below her. She was almost at the end of her strength. Strange, she remembered her spot which could not be far away to her right where the cliffs started to rise. It was where she'd sat the month before she'd married Peter. It all seemed so distant now. Oh, if only she could go back and re-live her life again. She wouldn't make so many terrible mistakes. She'd believed his every word and it was all falsehood and wicked, wicked lies.

She must have slept for a few minutes for when she came to herself, the first beams of steady light were picking out the few pink clouds high above her and it was light enough to see her way on down to the beach. Weakly, she pushed herself to her feet and painfully pressed on an erratic course down to where the sand and shingle met the trackway. The beach at last. She pulled off her shoes and walked slowly towards the edge of the water.

She realised that the bullying that had followed through her school life had affected her personality. There was no way it couldn't have. For years, fear ruled in her heart above every other emotion. It flowed over her in waves that threatened to drown her and there seemed to be no escape. Ever since Miss Hillem's attack she seemed to invite the adverse attention of those children who were older, bigger or stronger than she was. They had followed her home, hit her, kicked her, stolen her things, damaged her bicycle and laid in wait for her so they could attack her when she least expected it. By the end of that first term, she lived in constant fear with every waking moment a plea that they would leave her alone. He father died that Christmas holiday and her mother had problems of her own to cope with. She remembered the two of them, sitting holding each other and tearfully hoping that the new year would bring some happiness for both of them.

Needless to say, it didn't. The bullying persisted into her secondary school with one girl in particular making her life a misery. Her new form teacher Mr Wilson was a kindly man, full of enthusiasm and the children found him a welcome relief from Miss Hillem. They had taken to him even more after he confided to them that Miss Hillem had decided to take advice and leave the teaching profession. Apparently, the staff had found her impossible to work with and one or two had threatened to leave.

'Of course, I haven't said a word,' he smiled.

He'd tried to help with the bullying, but couldn't really deal with the things that happened outside school and when it became apparent that she'd confided in him, she had to endure the ensuing escalation. Even her few friends were lied to and intimidated ensuring that she remained isolated and vulnerable. Her work suffered and she took time off to wander alone in the lanes and woods that surrounded the town.

Sara was one of the last batch of pupils to sit for the School Certificate before the advent of the new General Certificate. She passed, though not with any distinctions as the school had expected. She left school despite the opportunity to enter the Sixth and qualify for a County Major Scholarship to university. Against advice, she took a job in a local firm of solicitors attending Night School to learn shorthand and typing. At least she'd left the torment behind and her inquisitor had gone to work for a wholesaler at the other end of the town.

When she was seventeen, her mother remarried and her stepfather Russell moved into the family house. At the same time she learned that her father had left her some money in trust until she was twenty one, when, apparently, she would be quite well set up with either a lump sum or an annuity large enough to manage comfortably on her own. These were the golden years. She became a proficient typist and on her twentieth birthday was appointed secretary to a partner in the firm. The situation at home was however becoming difficult. Her stepfather began to take more than a fatherly interest in her and started to look for every opportunity of being alone with her. At first it was a hand on her shoulder and then a stroking of her forearm during conversation.

Sara didn't know quite how to handle it. At first she pretended it hadn't happened and blamed an over active imagination. However, it soon developed into a cat and mouse game in which Sara would feel his eyes following her everywhere she went in the house. It needed only a quick glance to confirm she was right. Should she tell her mother and if she did what would be her mother's reaction? Matters reached a climax during the spring of the following year when Russell quietly entered her bedroom as she was preparing for bed. Sara had just bathed. Her mother was humming gently to herself in the kitchen below. Russell pushed her to the bed and clamped his hand across her face.

'Don't make a sound you teasing little bitch,' he mouthed.

Sara struggled frantically and managed to bite his hand.

He hit her.

She raised herself up on one elbow, her heart racing in panic Her breathing choked her.

'Cup of tea, love?' came a call from the bottom of the stairs.

Russell slipped out.

Sara bit her mouth to prevent herself from crying out.

'Thanks Mum.'

She knew then she had to leave. She'd said nothing to her mother and hoped for her sake that Russell would never hurt her though she feared that he would not be able to sustain any marriage with that side to his nature. Her flesh crawled whenever she thought of him and she feared for her mother. She wondered if Russell's love for her mother was genuine or fuelled by the thought of a comfortable house and a regular unearned income. She hoped her mother had been wise.

A fortnight later, Sara had taken a small rented flat quite close to her work and busied herself making it look homely and bright. That was when Peter had arrived in her life.

Peter was newly qualified and had joined the firm as a junior. From the outset he made a bee-line for Sara and neglected no opportunity to flatter her or go out of his way to pay her compliments. A few years older than herself, Peter was a tall, well-built, confident man who seemed proficient at his job and destined for great things. He laughed a lot, had a huge sense of humour and loved to be the life and soul of any gathering. Sara soon found herself looking forward to her daily meetings with him as he stopped to chat and have a joke. Before long they were going out regularly to the cinema, to concerts and for long walks on the local wolds. She found that she could relax in his company and gradually her fears subsided and she began to feel really confident for the first time in her life. Perhaps things would go right for her at last. As Peter learned more about her, she was delighted to find that he professed sensitivity too and he brought her poetry he'd written for her. He seemed to be the perfect gentleman and certainly the sort of person Sara could see herself settling down with. As Peter confided in her she learned that there were certain financial difficulties that impeded his genuine desire to make a home for them both. She was delighted to tell him that she was able to bring her own contribution to the relationship and they lost no time in planning arrangements to release Sara's inheritance for a future together. Her mother seemed pleased and thought Peter charming. Sara was a little nonplussed when she realised that settling the financial difficulties and putting a deposit on a new house on the edge of town had taken the lion's share of her portion but she comforted herself with the fact that she'd found the one person that could make her happy in life and she was content to share her all with him.

They'd come to Robin Hood's Bay that summer. It was a glorious time. The sun shone and they swung, hand in hand along the beach, oblivious of everything but the vibrant intimacy she felt with her husband to be. One evening, he left her, saying that he wanted to be alone to count his blessings at meeting so perfect a partner. She smilingly agreed and spent the evening walking slowly up the beach towards Mill Beck thinking how lucky she was to have met so lovely a man. He returned, a little unsteadily, late that night and let himself in without waking her. By morning, he was his old self.

She'd forgotten who it was that had said something to her the next day but she remembered how it had brought a frown to her face. Some remark about the the young man and his behaviour the previous evening. She dismissed it.

They were married at the local Registry Office. Neither seemed to have many friends and Peter's parents sent excuses that they were unable to be there. Peter seemed to be short of funds so Sara proposed that they spend their honeymoon in the locality, perhaps staying in a farmhouse. She would be happy with anywhere so long as they were together. Peter didn't seem to be happy with this and persuaded Sara to spend money she'd planned for the house on a trip abroad. In the end they'd gone to Paris and Sara paid for the flights and the hotel.

The physical act of coming together for the first time, something that they had both agreed would be a special occasion worth waiting for, was a shocking experience. Peter was clumsy and insensitive, leaving after minutes to go down to the bar. Sara cried.

As the days passed and turned into months, Peter gradually relaxed into the self-opinionated, selfish, unreliable, shallow person he was. The poetry he'd written for her wasn't his. The manners he displayed for others weren't given willingly to her any longer. The time he spent at home grew less and less and the glances she had from colleagues in the office showed pity rather than sympathy.

Was it only yesterday that the secretary to the senior partner had taken her aside and said that she really ought to share what she knew with her. Sara still didn't know what was about to be made plain to her. She'd worked with Miss Telford for years now and trusted her implicitly. Miss Telford had put her arm around Sara's shoulder and walked her down the corridor to the interview room. She shut the door.

'My dear,' she began, 'I don't know the easy way to tell you this but you will be the last person in the office to know what has been going on. Quite plainly, your Peter has been playing around with more than one young girl, spending more money than he earns and not presenting accounts that satisfy my boss. I'm afraid that the police will have to be brought in to investigate certain irregularities that amount to a considerable sum of money missing from the firm and it looks as if a paternity order is about to be served upon him by a young lady from his previous address.'

Sara collapsed.

It was then that she'd taken his car and driven wildly up the road to the junction at the end of the town.

The sand was cold and the fine, sea-tumbled beach gravel sharp to her feet. The sun swept up and blazed but she didn't see it. Her world, for which she had never been ready, had finally ended. She would never go back. Before she made her last great effort she vowed that she'd spend every summer here on the beach at Bay and that nothing, nothing would stand in her way.

A week later a short paragraph appeared in three national newspapers after which no further information seemed to be forthcoming.

> "A large sum of money is reported to be missing from a Sleaford firm of solicitors. Police are keen to trace solicitor Peter Sanderson whose black Austin 16 was discovered abandoned on the road between Scarborough and Whitby last month. Reports that Sanderson and a young woman had been seen in Southampton last Friday have been confirmed. Continental police have been alerted to look out for Mr and Mrs Sanderson."

An even shorter paragraph appeared in a September edition of the Daily Express.

> "No trace of solicitor Peter Sanderson or his wife Sara has been found. It has been confirmed that twenty thousand pounds is still missing from the Sleaford solicitors where Sanderson worked. Unconfirmed sightings have been reported in France and Italy."

CHAPTER THREE

'Well, how did your day go?' enquired Dick from his chair.

'Quite interesting actually,' returned Sylvia, dropping a brown paper bag on the table.

'This is for you. It came in with a box of books from the sale I was telling you about. You know, the one at Sandsend last week.'

Dick began to open the bag and was intrigued to discover a book he'd not seen since it was first published by a brother officer in 1947. It was about the part played by landing craft in all the major theatres of the war since their invention. It mentioned some of the exploits that he himself had taken part in when on 367 at Salerno, Augusta and Normandy.

'Well, fancy that. This has been out of print for decades and is quite rare. It was mentioned on the television only the other night but no-one had seen a copy.'

Sylvia smiled.

'That's not all; there was a man in the shop this afternoon asking about smuggling in the town. Pat just happened to come in and we had a most interesting chat about those days. She was telling us about the methods they used and how they used to frighten the townsfolk with stories of ghosts to guarantee a safe passage for their cargoes.'

'I thought the whole town was involved with smuggling,' said Dick. 'There'd be no need to go to all that effort.'

'There would always be things that were best not seen so they couldn't be talked about. Pat was telling this man about Linger's ghost and how it was set up. Apparently, a rider swathed in a white sheet and mounted on a horse with muffled hooves would appear descending Linger's Hill in the early dusk that preceded a run.'

'They were more gullible in those days,' retorted Dick.

'Then the talk got on to secret hiding places, tunnels and secret cellars.'

'Did you mention this cottage?' asked Dick. 'You know, the old hidden wall cupboard or our noisy ghost?'

'No,' laughed Sylvia. 'I don't think our cupboard was anything else but a cupboard. Besides, you'd never get a cask in there.'

'It would take lace or tobacco,' rejoined Dick, not wanting to lose the argument.

'Perhaps,' chuckled Sylvia.

'My colleague was telling us about the cottage where she lives. Apparently it has its unexplained story which could be counted as a ghost story or a most unusual occurrence. She was saying that only last month workmen were frightened by noises in there when everyone was out.'

Sylvia went on. 'The thing that baffles me is the difficulty in discerning between the country or urban myth and the personal experience of the observer.'

'You mean like the Flying Dutchman or the Vanishing Hitch-hiker stories. They keep on turning up. They have a long pedigree but always seem to have happened to a friend of a friend on some unrecorded day in the last month.'

'Yes. We looked at a story today that we found in The Somerset Year Book published in Taunton in 1927. It was almost word for word the same as a story that has been circulating here since the days of the fishing fleet.'

'Which one is that then?' enquired Dick, sitting back.

'Well, the Somerset version is based in the port of Minehead just after the turn of the century. The author, Clement Kille, was not specific about the exact date. It tells the story of a coasting skipper's walk up from the harbour to his cottage on the hill and how he fell in with a shipmate who was strangely reticent as they toiled upwards. It was the next morning before he was to learn that this particular shipmate had drowned in the harbour the previous night shortly before the captain had started his climb. The Bay version is very similar only the seamen are fishermen and not the crew of coasters. Another thing about the stories is the hidden identities of the actual participants. Kille uses false names and even his vessel names are not the names of any vessels regularly in Minehead harbour at the time. Its the same here in Bay. The names of the regular fisher families are never referred to and the street and house names are also disguised.'

'You might argue that that was done to protect the original teller of the tale and to deflect ridicule in a close community.'

'And you might argue that, as it is virtually impossible to pin either story down, they were both spin-offs from an earlier published tale or fireside story.'

Sylvia warmed to her subject. 'You see, these stories always contain a wealth of ambiguous detail, updated each decade with contemporary well-known facts to add veracity. As the years pass by, the names of the vessels or boats change as do the characters in the dramas. If you like, they are unending, open ended stories that preserve a central kernel that is readily accepted and easily digested.'

'So you don't think that the Flying Dutchman story has any basis in fact?' queried Dick.

'No. There's too many vessel types described for the story to remain constant. A ghostly image, if of a specific ship, must remain constant, or it fails to be the same vessel. The story likely to be a genuine experience is one that is seen by more than one person on a number of occasions and where the image remains the same in each case.'

'So Linger's ghost was an obvious invention and the story of the drowned fisherman climbing the Bank a long established myth that surfaces every now and again.'

'Right,' Sylvia smiled.

'I don't reckon you lot do any work at all up there in that shop. Its all yarning and drinking tea.'

'And finding books for idle husbands. I suppose you'll want a cup of tea now?'

'Thanks.' Dick looked up with a slow smile. 'I deserved that.'

Dick sighed and wondered if the time was right to reveal the vivid dreams of last night or his growing conviction that their ghost was not a myth or a fabrication designed to divert attention. For the moment, he thought that discretion would be the easiest course but felt in his bones that the time was fast coming when he could leave his sleeping dogs lying no longer. He often bumped into Pat and thought that it might be a good idea if he started a similar vein of conversation going. It might lead to a more sympathetic reception.

By eight o'clock, a warm almost tangible dusk had filled up the few irregular spaces between the cottages and the first orange lights were beginning to appear, first in the ground floor living spaces of the street dwellings and then in the higher houses as the last of the day filtered away against the strengthening outline of the high wooded confines of Bay. Dick reached out and switched on the brass table lamp and taking up the book was soon far back in his Royal Navy days as First Lieutenant of LST 367 at Salerno. The book, *Down Ramps*, by Lieutenant Lambton Burn RNVR, sketched over the times that were etched deeply into Dick's mind and touched briefly on incidents that he recalled all too well.

Sylvia looked out her airmail paper and began a letter to Pam. The cottage lapsed into a contented silence interrupted only by an involuntary grunt from Dick or the odd murmer from Sylvia as she wove her week into words and tried to condense the activities of Bay into an amusing monologue which would bring their worlds closer together. Of course she could have telephoned but old habits die hard and both Pam and Sylvia looked forward to the weekly letter in which their various, separated doings found substance in articulate, amusing and observant comments.

So deep were they both that they almost ignored the insistent jangle of the 'phone. Sylvia reached out from where she was sitting and answered automatically. Annie's voice.

'Mum, Annie.'

'Hello darling.'

'Mum, would it be alright if I came up to stay for a few days? I can get a lift tomorrow with a friend's husband and be in Whitby by midday. I'd love to see you both.'

'Of course, darling.'

'Could Dad pick me up on the bridge?'

'I'm sure that will be fine. How are the boys?'

'They are going to London to visit their father which is why I thought I might take a break too and come up to see you.'

'We'll look forward to it. See you tomorrow then.'

'That's lovely. Bye.'

'Bye darling.'

Sylvia looked across to Dick.

'Annie's coming up tomorrow. She wants to know if you can pick her up tomorrow on the bridge.'

Dick smiled as several thoughts crossed his mind at the same time He could drive in a bit earlier, stroll on down the quayside and have a look at the fishing boats, pop in for a pint, and perhaps talk to his daughter about his visitor. She was interested in the paranormal and belonged to a group that had investigated several unusual happenings in the town where she lived. He'd only half listened before when she'd tried to tell them about a particular house in the town that appeared to have a similar problem. He thought he remembered that the outcome had been satisfactory.

'That 'll be fine,' he nodded.

They'd worked the bridge routine many times before. Annie would wait at the traffic lights on the town side of the bridge and wave as he drove over. Then it was a case of driving on around the roundabout by the station and she would jump in at the lights before driving out for Bay. Only this time he would leave the car in the car park on the left as he drove in and walk. Annie loved to walk around Whitby so the two of them could take an hour or two and have a chat.

Feeling more settled, Dick returned to his book and was soon thinking that he could have added several interesting stories to the narrative. Perhaps he ought to write something one day. Sylvia, the real scribe of the family, was already half way down her third page.

The next day dawned cold and blustery but by the time Dick had breakfasted, idly glanced at the paper, cleared away and bid a goodbye to Sylvia, the light had increased and there was a promise of sunshine somewhere up there among the long grey streamers.

'If the weather improves it will be fine for a walk out on the breakwater and if it doesn't there might just be something that Annie could listen to, that is if she could hear it,' Dick murmured to himself.

The next job was to get the car out. This was the only drawback to living in Bay. Before the yellow lines, it was almost impossible to get a car round into King Street unless one tackled it early in the day before the inevitable visitor had confidently decided he could climb up from the Dock and turn left into Chapel Street at the top. Back down they had to come in reverse and if they found someone had parked outside the Dolphin, then it was a case of sitting it out for a while. Even with the lines it was still bad on occasions when the brewery lorry blocked the road or the Dock was crammed with day visitors who thought they could escape the lines by jamming up the slope under Coble Heads and even up the private access by the side of the old Post Office. Dick had long since abandoned any thoughts of driving his antique motor down the Bank and around the Dock. It was too much trouble so he kept his car by arrangement with a friend who lived in Mount Pleasant. They shared the drive but even here there was sometimes trouble as someone heedlessly blocked them both in. Bay wasn't designed for motor cars and the number of interesting situations that developed almost daily in the summer was a constant topic of conversation.

He didn't really mind the walk up. It was excellent exercise and there were several ways up so it was a rare walk without stopping to have a word with someone. Today the drive was clear and Bill had switched the cars around so he could drive straight out. They both had keys so that they could make life easier for each other. They had jokingly agreed that each switch would cost a pint and it had worked very well to date.

To say that Dick's car was antique was no joke. It was a pre-war Lanchester of the fluid flywheel variety in original faded black splashed carelessly with essence of herring gull. Dick had got used to it and it had never let him down. Folk were always telling him to have it restored but he didn't want a museum exhibit, he wanted a car and it fitted him like an old pair of slippers.

The car park he'd thought of was full but he managed to barge in at the roadside. There was over an hour before he needed to look out for Annie so he thought he'd do his usual thing which entailed looking at the vessels that were in and strolling up to the fish quay to take in the latest developments in fishing boat design. They had changed out of all recognition since the war years. He remembered the names of some of the local strongly built wooden keel-boats. There was the *Provider, North Star, Gem, Pilot Me* and *Victory Rose.* Then in the fifties and sixties came some magnificent wooden motor seiners from the east coast Scottish ports. The stubby vessels of the nineties with their turtle-backed shelters completely enclosing the foredeck might be more comfortable to work in but the lines didn't appeal. He wondered what kind of sea boats they were. As he retraced his steps he was pleased to see that cobles were still in evidence and several of the large half-decked variety were secured alongside.

That done, he turned back and headed for the little picture gallery in the station building. He'd bought a watercolour from there last year and always kept an eye open for pictures of ships that might fit into the cottage.

It turned out to be one of those intuitive moves as in the window he spotted a small oil painting showing a pair of half-decked cobles identical to the ones he'd been looking at. They were skilfully and carefully done and appealed to the sailor in him.

After browsing about in there for a while he set off for his rendezvous with a flat brown paper parcel tucked under his arm. He was rehearsing the comment he might make to introduce his latest acquisition when it crossed his mind that he might creep up behind his daughter as she looked out across the bridge waiting for his well-known motor. He soon spotted her wearing a blue duffle coat with a splash of scarlet about her neck. Her head was bare and her brown hair fell about her shoulders. She carried an aura of confidence and he felt the warmth of pride rise within him. Annie was a hugely practical, capable and imaginative person who had survived several disasters that would have wrecked a lesser character. She had a buoyant sense of humour and a ready sense of fun that had ridden out the storms of her marriage break-up and the subsequent dealings with her unthinking ex-partner. She was a strong, intuitive, intelligent girl. True to his plan, Dick stole up behind her and tapped her on the shoulder. Annie swung around.

'Oh, hi Dad!'

'Hello dear, nice to see you. You're looking well.'

'How are you Dad? Mum OK?'

'Fine thanks. I thought we'd take a stroll while we're here, there's something I want to talk about. Do you fancy a beer?'

'Desperately. I've been in a car for three and a half hours and I'm gasping.'

They linked arms and sauntered back up the quayside.

'You should have been here earlier this summer. The *Endeavour* paid us a visit and the whole district turned out to welcome her. You've never seen such a crowd. There were tens of thousands crowding the harbour and cliffs. As she came in she fired a salute and sailed majestically past here through the bridge to tie up close to where the original was built. The queues to go on board her were hours long and the town has never been so crowded.'

'Did you manage to get on board?'

Dick smiled and winked. 'I happened to know one of the people who were guiding visitors around and they were allowed to invite a guest, so I managed to get on board without queueing.'

'Trust you.'

'I got some brilliant photos. I'll show you when we get home.'

They turned into the Jolly Sailors and were soon sitting behind a couple of pints.

'Now, what was it you wanted to talk about?'

Annie put her head on one side and looked inquisitively at her father. It was a rare occasion when he said he wanted to talk rather than chat so there must be something on his mind. She wondered if everything was alright at home.

'Back home at Leek,' he started, 'you belong to a group that investigates the paranormal.'

'Yes. The Green Dragon Mysteries Society. We meet once a month and listen to speakers from all over the country. We have all sorts who belong. Mediums, dowsers, clairvoyants, astrologists, ufologists and the like. We have a very varied programme so that members can choose which talks to come along to. We've had everything from aura photography and map dowsing to bible analysis and abductions. Some of it's a bit way out but there's always something for everyone.'

'And what are you interested in?'

'Well, I belong to a small group of people who are sometimes asked to go and have a look at supposedly haunted houses.'

'What do you do?'

'Basically, we ascertain whether or not there is anything there and if there is, we see if we can help.'

'How can you tell if there is really someone there? I mean someone could tell you any old rubbish.'

'Oh yes, they often do.'

'Well, how can you actually tell whether or not the whole thing is a fake? How can you tell if someone has had a real experience?'

'There are several ways. In our group we have a dowser, a medium and a sensitive who can actually "see" if there is anything there. That way we can correlate our findings and agree when, for instance, the sensitive person "sees" a figure and the dowser gets a reaction from the same place.'

'What part do you play?'

'I use dowsing tools, a rod and a pendulum and they give me a physical reaction to an actual stimulus.'

Dick took another swallow and wondered what he was getting into. This was out of his territory although he had heard of water divining and he knew that worked because he had seen it used only recently by a local Water Board man.

'Do you have a hazel twig or two metal wires that cross over like a water diviner?' he asked.

'It's a bit like that, only I use a smaller more sophisticated rod. It's about three inches long and set in bearings to make it more sensitive.'

'What is the difference between dowsing and water divining then?'

'Very little really. It's all a matter of what you are looking for. Dowsing is a discipline stemming from practice. It's an active interrogative. The mind seeks rather like a a radio set tuning to a particular station and rejecting all the other incoming signals.'

'It's a bit like picking up a radio wave then?' enquired Dick.

'Exactly. The dowser seeks for a particular signal and gets a twitch when he finds it. So, to get back to the original question, if there is really a presence in a particular place, the dowser will find it. The opposite is also true. No presence, no signal.'

'So if there is a long term presence in a particular place, you could tell me whether or not it was imagination.'

'Yes. I think I could. Why? Is there something you've discovered in the cottage? I don't think I ever experienced anything in the weeks when I've been there.'

'It isn't anything that happens in the summer much and in the old days when I was in and out of the place I can't say I noticed it much either. However I'd be grateful if you'd have a look for me when we get back. You could have a go before your mother gets home. I don't want to upset her. There's no need to say anything at this stage.'

'Right, I'll have a go for you.'

'There's a chap who gets in the Dolphin occasionally. He has one of these divining things. He's found some coins on the beach with it though it beats me how he does it. When he's in Bay he stays with Pat up the road. She's the friend who got me onto the *Endeavour*. I think he's been coming to Bay since the mid sixties. In fact I'm sure I spotted him this morning as I was walking up.'

'I'd like to meet him. We dowsers like to compare notes. We all seem to specialise in different aspects. There's dowsing and healing, dowsing to find lost or missing objects, dowsing for archaeological remains or for minerals, map dowsing and dowsing to measure the effect of radiation or electrical energy from wires and cables. It's a huge area.'

'Have you got your dowsing kit with you? asked Dick.

'Always carry it with me,' Annie smiled. 'You never know when it will be wanted.'

She opened her shoulder bag and produced a small shiny angle of brass about four inches long and a tiny leather bag containing a crystal on the end of a thread.

'Does it really do all those things?'

'Its not the tool that does it, it's the person. The tool is only the indicator or the needle on the dial if you like.'

Dick picked up the rod and turned it around in his hand.

'How does it work?' he pressed.

'I'll show you later,' she grinned, 'after you've allowed me to have that drink you bought me.'
Annie lifted her pint and took a long, cool drink.
'There, I've been waiting for that!'
Dick smiled ruefully and pushed the rod back across the table to his daughter. It seemed as if Annie would be able to help him discover whether or not there was anything in the cottage. He looked forward to the results.

CHAPTER FOUR

Within the hour they had tucked the Lanchester away in Mount Pleasant and were legging it down the Bank among the loitering visitors looking into the windows of the shops and cottages alike. They turned left into Chapel Street, Annie noticing the differences since her last visit. The pottery at the bottom of the Openings had closed and a bookshop opened in its stead. She was delighted that the antique shop Valeriana was still there. They'd always got Leo Walmsley books in stock and she'd collected nearly all of them. She'd love to have one of his father's paintings but they were getting very expensive even if you could find one nowadays. She'd made do with some of his postcards which were easier on the pocket. Dick looked in there for cameras as he had an interest in old folding Kodaks and Sylvia often popped in on her way home from work or in the lunch break to see if there were any interesting items of Victorian cutlery.

They passed the chapel which had been lovingly restored by Leon and Pat Labistour some years ago. On several occasions the whole family had been to concerts in the intimate auditorium preserved within the old building. They were a delight but had ceased when the building was sold and changed into a bookshop and tea room. On her last visit, Annie had browsed among the disorganised heaps of books that seemed to jumble from every shelf and corner before settling for a book of poetry and a cup of tea in the tea room behind the shop. Some remnants of Leon's model of the cliff town had survived but little fingers had managed to effect as much damage as the gales of the centuries had on the real Bay. Dick thought that the place had changed hands again and that the new owners had plans for starting up the concerts again.

Right into King Street and the cottage in sight. A glimpse over the sea wall across the space beside Seascape revealed a rising tide with masses of grey-white water flecking the ends of the scaurs. Aggressive puffs of wind seemed almost certain to increase into the gusts that had only recently died away. It was one of those uncertain Autumn days when the first tastes of change were beginning to be noticed. The vestiges of blue had vanished from the sky and there was a definite chill in the air. Dick wondered whether or not to mention that the ghost of a tall, dark seafarer wrapped in a boat cloak had been seen looking out to sea from this spot but stopped himself, felt for his key and the pair of them were soon inside the familiar walls. Annie's nostalgia was as potent as ever as she fondly stepped again into the cottage where she'd spent so many happy summer holidays as a child. It was the little things really. The curly iron hook on the back of the front door which she'd had difficulty in reaching. The tiny square recess in the stone wall which had been a cupboard in the panelling before her father had stripped it out and the old rug in front of the fire which had been a part of her life ever since she could remember. Where had the years gone? For longer than a second she could believe that the years that stood between had fled away and she was here as a young girl before her troubles began. In so many ways she felt the same but in so many others she knew the price of her maturity.

The parlour was much the same. The model of the corvette *Myosotis* was still wanting a case and was as dusty as she remembered, no-one having dared to touch it. Rows of books about the sea filled the low bookcase and the prized nautical impedimenta seemed to be as much in evidence as always, a tribute to her mother's patience or indulgence.

'I'll take my bag up Dad,' she called.

Dick put his head around the kitchen door.

'You're in your old room.'

Annie caught up her bag by the shoulder strap and started up the narrow twisting stairwell which surely owed its origins to the time when there was a central post with rungs hammered into it in an ascending spiral. Her room was right at the top with a small dormer overlooking the roofs and chimneys of the neighbouring cottages. She walked across the sloping floorboards and looked out. A few feet to her left, a herring gull's nest was glued haphazardly to the small ledge half way up next door's chimney stack. She would be assured of Bay music at the first glimmer of light. Never any need of alarm clocks here. Turning back she caught sight of Jennifer, her doll tucked into the fold of the duvet cover.

'Bless you Mum,' she thought.

She dropped her duffle coat across the foot of the bed and taking her dowsing rod from the side pocket of her bag she went back downstairs to see what her father was anxious about. As she ducked into the parlour she saw a tray with two mugs of tea on the gateleg table. Dick was sitting smiling up at her. There was no sign of the brown paper parcel he'd been carrying.

'You've got your thing with you, I hope.'

Annie put the rod on the table and reached for her tea.

'First things first,' she said.

'You don't mind me asking?'

'Not at all. Look, I'll treat you as a client and we'll do this professionally. First I'll try to explain what a ghost is.'

Annie stretched out in her mother's chair and took a swift gulp of tea.

'The usual report is the claim that the subject has received a sensory experience that indicates a presence. This is the primary way in which someone indicates that they have experienced something out of the ordinary. Some claim that they have seen a figure, some have heard a voice and others have felt a strong sense that they are not alone. Some folk admit to smelling the distinct odour of clothing or tobacco, scent or hair oil. It is now accepted that in the so called "ghost" experience, a package or collection of particular data, is received directly by the brain which leaves the brain with the problem of how it came to be there. The only way it can be described is that it was sensed in the normal way. It is not always the case that subjects receive data from a particular presence in the same way. One will claim sight, another sound and another might just feel uneasy or that they are being watched.'

'I know what you mean about that; being watched. I definitely get that feeling here, especially when its stormy weather outside.'

'What other indications have you had that might be described as unusual or odd?'

'Well,' started Dick, 'It was sounds at first, but only when the conditions were right. It 's usually associated with a storm or rough weather in the Bay. I get the feeling it's an old chap. It's almost as if he was at my shoulder sometimes.'

'Has Mum heard anything?'

'Not that she's said but I haven't really told her the details. She does know the difference between stories and actual experiences. We've talked about that.'

'Well Dad, it sounds as if you have got a presence and one who has managed to get quite close to you. Have you ever seen anything?'

'Only in that half-way state beween sleeping and waking when its not certain whether you are dreaming or not.'

'Yes, that's a well recognised state of relaxation when we can become very receptive.'

'Do you believe in spirits then, Annie?'

Annie smiled.

'Like many other declarations of belief it depends very much on your understanding of the concept in question. I believe in the ability of the human mind to survive the experience we call death and in certain relevant circumstances to communicate or attempt to communicate where there is need. An experience of such a mind is often no more than being receptive to the concern or pressing wish of a human being that has passed through the barrier of death. Mostly we can help but not always.'

'How can we know what they want?' persisted Dick.

'In a nutshell, by a receptive, compassionate and empathetic dialogue using the skills of a sensitive, a medium or a dowser. The problem is there and someone has gone to a great deal of effort to make contact. It is often only our dullness or set ideas that prevent a satisfactory ending to the matter.'

'Do you ever go on ghost hunts with some of the more well known groups?'

'Definitely not. Most so called ghost hunters are still looking on a physical level with electrical and photographic instruments not understanding that the data or references are on a mental level. Others are simply looking to satisfy their curiosity. We only become involved if there is a genuine need and use the tools I mentioned, sensitivity, empathy and compassion. Above all, compassion. Most apparitions are creatures of emotion and it is with that faculty of mind they are understood and helped. It takes a human to help a human despite the passage of time in our world. One of the reasons that there are so many ghosts around is the legacy of fixed ideas the sprang from religion and the emergence of so called science.'

Annie rose to her feet and took up her dowsing rod.

'There's no need for this really. I can operate without it but when you see it working in my hand, it will show you whether your feelings have been confirmed by another.'

Dick started to get up.

'Stay there Dad. I'll dowse and tell you where the signal is strongest. Then when I'm close I'll use the pendulum and ask some questions.'

Annie closed her eyes for a moment and relaxed. Then holding the rod in her hand, she moved slowly across the room with the pointer extended before her. As she passed the fireplace, the pointer jerked around and on the left of the chimney breast it repeated the movement. She put the rod down and took the pendulum from her pocket. Then sitting quietly she set it gently swinging to and fro, checking it again and again from circling in an anti-clockwise direction. After what seemed an age she nodded and looked up.

'You've definitely got a presence here and someone who has lived here for a very long time. He's a seaman with a lot of years at sea and he has a strong desire to make contact with you about a private and personal matter. I felt him by the fireside here and would imagine that it was a favourite spot.'

'How can you tell all that by just walking across the room?'

Dick still felt a little uneasy. He'd lived in a shell of familiar proven realities where science was certain of what was possible. His religious upbringing had also told him that when you were dead you went to heaven or hell and that there was no way of making contact ever again. The idea of a consciousness surviving death and attempting to make contact with the living was a bit much to swallow. Yet he had to admit to the experiences he'd had in this cottage.

'It's a matter of opening the mind and posing the right questions. Dowsing is all sensitive, intelligent questioning.'

'What on earth does he want with me?' puzzled Dick.

'That's for you to discover now that you know for certain that someone from the past has something he wants to tell you.'

'How should I set about it?' asked Dick.

'I think you already have when you caught a glimpse of him across the fireside. Remember, it's not your eyesight that is involved, it's the mind so try to relax and become receptive to ideas. It's difficult if you've never done it intentionally but persevere and I'm sure you'll find the way. Most folk still only catch that quick image and then their sense of reality steps in and they overcome it.'

Dick pursed his lips and thought quietly for a few minutes. He'd never realised that Annie had looked into these things so deeply and had reached such conclusions. On the surface it seemed to make sense. He recollected a story he'd heard on board his LST when it was fitted out as a hospital ship ferrying casualties back to the UK from the Normandy battles. An SBA had related how he'd talked to a badly wounded Marine on a stretcher waiting to be taken on board and comforted him. The Marine had said that he owed his mother a pound and would he please go and give it to her. It was a Mrs Bassett at Raleigh Road, Exeter. In the short hours that preceded docking the Tiffy had forgotten to collect the pound but by coincidence lived in Exeter and not far from Raleigh Road. On his next leave he decided to call and see how the Marine had fared. He duly found Mrs Bassett who sadly told him that her son had been reported killed in action on the first day. Convinced he wasn't mistaken he told her that he'd met her son on the other side of the Channel and that he'd been concerned that he'd owed her a pound. Mrs Bassett said that her son had indeed borrowed a pound on the last day of his leave and had promised faithfully to pay it back. The SBA handed her a pound note but failed to tell her that their meeting must have taken place a month after her son had been killed. It seemed a trivial matter to be concerned about but it must have been on the poor man's mind as he died.

Annie broke the silence.

'What time will Mum be getting home?

Dick looked at his watch.

'Any time now. I think we'll put the kettle on. No need to tell your mother you've developed into a witch so we won't mention any of this.'

The kettle had only just boiled when the door opened and Sylvia entered with a carrier bag.

'There,' she smiled, continuing through to the kitchen. 'We can have a good dinner together and catch up on all the news.'

Annie put her arms around her mother and gave her a kiss. It was always good to be together and they'd not had the opportunity to have a good chatter for months.

'Did you have a good journey up?'

'Yes thanks. I came up with a friend's husband who had a meeting in Whitby this afternoon. He's been looking for business opportunities in seaside towns where he can sell some of his firm's pottery. The company has recently developed a nautical range but is keen that it stays fairly exclusive and distinctive and doesn't become just more tourist junk. So far it is selling in just one outlet in Plymouth, Portsmouth, Falmouth, Bournemouth and Boston. They are looking at possibilities of moving north.'

'Whitby would be ideal,' said Sylvia. 'They had over a million visitors last year and it offers something to every possible taste. Art, music, drama and plenty of places to suit those who are interested in history or heritage.'

'He was worried that there might not be as much spare cash about as there is down south.'

'He's got a point. Even though there's more money about than there used to be, it's still a case of practicalities before frivolities up here,' returned Sylvia. 'But if it's a quality product, it should sell well wherever it is marketed. Folk will always have an eye for quality. Did you see any of it?'

'Yes. It was distinctive but a bit on the pricy side for me. The pottery industry is going through a rough patch at the moment mainly due to the strong pound and the fact that so much of it goes abroad.'

The two girls went through into the kitchen and emptied the carrier at which both minds started to be creative. With a bottle of good wine, it looked as if it would be an enjoyable evening.

Sylvia turned to her daughter.

'Look, let me do this. You take your Dad out for a while. He spends far too much time sitting down with his books and doesn't get half enough exercise. Oh I know he was out today but that was a rare occasion. You could get up the beach for a bit and when he's had enough buy him a pint in the Bay Hotel. Get him to tell you about his ghost.'

'What ghost?' quizzed Annie innocently.

'Lately he's been very interested whenever I've mentioned myths legends or ghosts and I suspect that he might have had an experience that he couldn't understand.'

'In here?'

'Well, he spends most of his time in here so I expect it must be, though I can't say that I've seen or heard anything out of the ordinary. He was up in the night a couple of times recently and I found him asleep in front of the fire. Something must have woken him.'

'Are you sure that you don't want any help?'

'No. You know what they say about two women in the kitchen. We'll talk later.'

Annie walked back into the parlour.

'We're under orders,' she smiled. 'We are to go out until Mum's had a chance to get dinner on the table. I must say that I'd enjoy some fresh air on the beach. Are you coming?'

Dick didn't like to pass up the opportunity of talking further and thought that this was perhaps the one occasion when he would exchange the warmth of his chair for a breezy beach. Annie went up for her coat and Dick collected his from the back of the door.

Soon the two of them were picking their way over the steep edge of the slip and finding the softer ground between the boulders and patches of shifting shingle. Far Ravenscar was partially obscured by a driven sea mist that had increased with the tide. It was still gusting with an occasional fine spatter of carried spray from the scaurs. There was under an hour of walking, perhaps half that would be safer. They took the higher way at the base of the grotesque piles of tumbled clay that marked the end of the land before the lias cliffs asserted themselves. Underfoot they came on piles of dried out seaweed in great straggling banks where the recent tides had swept them out of reach of the neaps. There was litter enough too among the more acceptable dunnage and scraps of discarded timber. The sky was looking angry, more so than before and Dick reckoned that they were in for another stormy night.

Despite his reluctance to admit it, Dick had been excited at the prospect of finding out more about his visitor although if Annie was right it was he who was the newcomer if the old chap had been a previous owner. He was about to broach the subject again when Annie spoke.

'You must have heard lots of stories of this coast since you've been here. Were any of them ghost stories?'

'Bless you, yes, there's dozens about these parts but, as your mother says, you have to be careful whether or not they are real experiences or just long term myths or silly stories made up to amuse the visitors.'

'What was the first one you heard?'

'That's easy. It was in Whitby. I was still a Lieutenant Commander in the Royal Navy then so it must have been just after the the war, perhaps 1947. I got to know a lady called Dora Walker who had a fishing boat in the harbour. She fished right through the war and was a well known local character. She was a great collector of model boats and I remember going to see her on more than one occasion. She also had an amazing collection of nautical things from charts to scrimshaw.'

'More than you?' teased Annie.

'Oh, much more, and far more interesting, for instance on one occasion she showed me an ebony walking stick that had once belonged to Nelson. Well, one day we were talking about the strange things that can happen at sea and she told me that before the war she and Laurence Mirfield were asked to go out to pick up some gear that had been left at sea following the loss of a Scarborough man from a coble. After searching, the skipper had made back into Whitby. He reported the man missing and then asked Dora if she'd go out for the gear. She'd agreed and after a longish search they found the gear but had the greatest difficulty hauling it. It proved desperately heavy and well nigh impossible to get inboard. Mirfield thought it was the dead man and spoke out for him after which the gear came in easily and they made a speedy passage into Whitby just before a storm broke. She was always puzzled about that.'

'Nothing was seen then?' asked Annie.

'Not in that story though I believed her implicitly. She was a well respected lady and not one for telling lies. Something unusual had happened for certain.'

'What about when you were at sea? Did you ever experience anything that could be called supernatural?'

'Well, Dora's story prompts me to remember how we lost a man over the side on a particularly nasty night. We searched for an hour but it was hopeless and he wouldn't have survived for long in the latitude we were in. The strange thing was when we got back into the Mersey and the order was given for special sea dutymen to close up, the missing man was seen making his way along the deck to go to his station. Several of his shipmates saw him and the skipper remarked "Isn't that Perkins?" There he was as large as life and as solid as the rest of us. In a minute or two he just faded away.'

'That's a more typical story.' She glanced at her watch.

'Hadn't we better think of turning back? I don't know about you but I'm beginning to feel a bit cold.'

They turned and found it easier with the stiffening wind behind them. Urged on from miles out, a lumpy, ragged tide made strongly up the beach sweeping the few remaining folk further and further back towards the slip. They would be about the last to get up.

'I think we've just got time for a quick one,' smiled Dick as they pressed on up the rough cobbles to the Dock.

As they did so they passed a tall, slim white-haired man standing by the railings looking out across the Bay. He was wearing an old faded blue gansey and a pair of light coloured trousers. His even features carried an air of concerned preoccupation as if watching for something far up the Bay. Dick spoke to him.

'Hello Michael. Looks like we're in for a blow.'

'Hello Dick. Yes, I think the tide will be well up the slip tonight.'

'Michael, this is my daughter Annie. She's staying for a few days.'

Annie turned and met a pair of intelligent blue-green eyes and a barely perceptible smile.

'Hello Annie. I'm sure that I've seen you about Bay before.'

'You have indeed, but not as much as I'd like. It's a place I've always loved.'

'Me too. I come when I can.'

Dick took his daughter's arm.

'We're going in The Bay for a few minutes before dinner. Would you care to join us?'

'That's kind of you but I have an appointment. Perhaps we'll bump into each other again before you go. Bye for now Annie, Dick.'

Michael turned back to gaze again up the Bay and the fleeting smile that had crossed his face for a second or two was drowned by an inner silence.

Dick inclined his head confidentially as they climbed up the steps to the door.

'That was the chap I was telling you about. The diviner.'

At the last minute Annie glanced back to take in the solitary figure standing at the rail. He too turned his head and for an all too brief moment their eyes met.

Dick was talking again.

'If we are in for a blow tonight, perhaps we will both be aware of this sailor chap. Shall I call you if I hear anything?'

CHAPTER FIVE

Michael John Cowlishaw was considering retirement. He thought that it might be here in Robin Hood's Bay but he still had a small Victorian terraced house in Oxford where he was a lecturer. That would have to go first. He'd thought of putting it on the market earlier in the spring but the prospect of clearing out many years of accumulated books, journals and files, to say nothing of his own researches which filled the shelves of two rooms, was mind blowing. He simply could not stop hoarding any interesting snippets that came his way and passing a bookshop was an impossibility. Some of his best finds had been in cardboard boxes of throw-outs from bookshops. If he did come up here it would mean finding a place big enough to store all his work and small enough to remain affordable.

Michael lectured in European History but his research was all confined to a period of the second world war when the elusive, and later mythic, British spirit was so painstakingly constructed. He'd managed to find some rare political pamphlets and documents which had set him on the trail and he'd never really strayed off it. His work had been recognised as valuable to those who sought to manipulate opinion in times of social stress and, to his surprise, he had been invited to attend a number of meetings with senior government ministers.

These he had always declined with appropriate thanks but he had spotted some unusual figures in his lectures from time to time and his books had always sold well. Of course he had found some answers to some old puzzles but the nugget of gold he came across a dozen or so years ago he'd kept to himself, packed away in the files in the back bedroom.

Michael had been married after what has been termed a whirlwind courtship during his first appointment at Bristol University. Celia had been lecturing there too and for a few months the situation had seemed idyllic. However it wasn't long before their careers tugged in different directions and Celia took up an offer of a post in California. Although she wrote regularly at first the letters tailed off and stopped altogether after she had decided that their marriage had been a mistake. Upon reflection Michael had realised that they had very little in common. Celia had no interest in taking academic subjects into her private life, something that Michael loved doing. Divorce was inevitable and perhaps best sooner than later. It had been decades since he'd heard from her.

It was 1960 when he'd first come up to Bay. He'd been on a painting holiday with a colleague from the Art School. They had decided that they would drive around the coast of England and Wales stopping wherever the muse directed. In the first weeks they'd crawled along the south coast, by-passed the Thames estuary and set out around the bulge of East Anglia stopping at the most unlikely and out of the way places to draw, paint, write and explore. His friend, Peter, was a brilliant artist and enthused about everything from the quality of light to the

wonderful landscapes and sunsets they found along that coast. Michael loved the buildings and the few unspoiled examples of vernacular architecture they stumbled on in small villages and towns they'd never heard of. As the holiday progressed, they became more and more involved until they ran out of Lincolnshire and found themselves for the first time browsing up the Yorkshire coast. A week later found them in Whitby where they stayed for a while. Finding Whitby for the first time was a delight and a surprise. It was a gem. After wishing for more hours in the day than there were, on recommendation they'd reluctantly moved back a few miles to see Robin Hood's Bay before heading on up the coast to Staithes and Redcar.

Of course that was the rest of the holiday finished for although they did finally leave Bay and carry on via Hadrian's Wall to the west coast and so on down to Bristol, they never forgot the magic of the day they first started to descend the Bank into that beautifully preserved time capsule that had somehow managed to escape the vandalism that was sweeping old buildings away in every city and town in the kingdom and replacing them with long lines of fresh concrete and glass. Right next to his rooms in Kingsdown, Bristol, they were, that very year, pulling down rows of elegant Georgian houses. But here, all was as it was when built and the result was not the single vernacular building rarely sandwiched but a total vernacular experience, a visit to the past where tasteful repairs and renovations had not destroyed the vibrant ambience of the whole. Michael could hardly believe his eyes and the two of them wandered about taking in the streets, doorways, windows and chimneys, the alleys and courts and the steps. Not only was the place a marvel for all to wonder at, it was heaven for a history graduate and there promised to be a rich heritage to be explored, artistically as well as historically.

Later that year Michael returned to stay with friends he had made in the town. They were artists and craftsfolk who had just taken a cottage at the top of King Street. Property was cheaper in those days but particularly so on the seaward side of King Street where the cliff was gradually slipping several feet a year into the sea. It seemed that the cottage in question had only a matter of a few years left before it too crashed over the edge. Huge cracks had already appeared in the cottage next door. No one dared believe at the time that a massive sea wall would save the street from the fate that had already claimed the rest of the road that climbed upwards out of the town. But the miracle happened.

It was on that visit that he'd had the experience that had altered his perspective on life. As an historian he was convinced of the necessity for strong primary evidence where any view of the past was concerned. Even his understanding of the present scene, social or political, had to be seen against a global background rather than from an individualistic construct or even a popular nationalistic standpoint. This desire to identify black and white in evidence tended to create in him a dogmatic approach to reality. Like a popular television programme of today he believed that the truth was out there, it only needed a persistent, inquisitive discipline to unearth and establish it. Safe in his real world, it came as a solid shock to discover that some things defied explanation.

It had all started on a warm September afternoon when he'd decided to walk up the beach towards Ravenscar. The day had been fine and the sea calm. There weren't many visitors about and he was soon way ahead of the most adventurous group who had set up camp high on the shingle underneath the boulder clay cliffs.

He was just congratulating himself that he was lord of all that he surveyed when a young woman walked up the beach from left to right about fifty yards ahead of him. There was nothing unusual about that except that he hadn't noticed her when he'd searched the beach ahead of him only seconds ago. He glanced towards the tide's edge from which direction she had appeared to have come and then back to the figure again. Where she should have been, now only thirty yards or so away, there was nothing. He was just telling himself that he'd probably seen a mirage, a cloud shadow or a trick of the light when she appeared again. He caught the movement in the corner of his eye and turned to watch her as again she walked purposefully from his left, across his path and up towards the cliff. This time he followed her movements carefully. As she passed in front of him for the second time he had the opportunity of observing her in detail. He was not in the habit of staring at girls and would normally have felt embarrassed to do so but on this occasion his curiosity was aroused. Here was a young lady who must have doubled back to repeat walking a sector of beach and she'd done it with incredible speed. He stopped.

She was in her late teens or early twenties and had striking good looks despite a certain vulnerability which was apparent in her open and candid expression. Her eyes were eager yet sad, bright yet wounded and he was immediately prompted to ask himself how she transmitted so much in so short a time. As she passed, he smiled involuntarily and hoped he'd conveyed encouragement. Perhaps she needed it. It was after she'd again slipped out of sight he deliberately searched for her with no success.

In retrospect, perhaps this first sighting hadn't registered quite so dramatically but in the light of subsequent incidents he knew that it had marked the beginning of the saga he'd become increasingly deeply involved in over the years that followed and quite unable to share.

The very next day he was down there again, intending to walk up to the stream bed where banks of fine shingle hid coloured quartz, jaspers, carnelian and emerald. These semi-precious stones weren't local, they'd been transported down the coast by longshore drift and the prevailing currents and tide patterns. Some were from as far away as Scotland whilst examples from Northumberland and Durham were also identified. Once embayed within headlands they became trapped, graded and sifted to form finely constituted gravel beds along with a million million other fragments of rocks and minerals. He'd found some beautiful emeralds and dozens of shades of carnelian. These gemstones were a bit like the more discerning visitors, once they'd discovered Bay, they tended to stay there.

On this mile or so of beach he knew he'd found the delight that Byron once wrote of when he said:

" There is a rapture on this lonely shore,
There is society where none intrudes,
By the deep sea, and music in its roar."

He had the best of both worlds here, the tangible legacy of the town and the more transient attractions of the beach. Both were very special places.

The patient exercise of pebble hunting was not far removed from that of historical research. Both took time and both were, in his eyes, equally enjoyable. On a warmish day he'd sit on a square of canvas and carefully peruse each handscoop slowly filling a pocket with possibles. He'd test them later. He remembered the old man who'd told him how to find the translucent ones and how to discover where the likely rarer stones were. He'd told him to walk with a low sun right in his face keeping his eyes on the wet shingle about three or four yards in front of him. Light would sparkle up from the translucent stones as they caught the suns rays and show him where they were. Ideal conditions were rare as a falling tide did not always coincide with a low sun but over the years he had discovered that all the brilliant sparkles were concentrated in a particular section of beach and now he seldom left the foreshore without a good carnelian or emerald in his pocket.

He'd been sitting for about half an hour scooping up handfuls of wet, beach-tumbled fragments and spreading them across his palm. Every now and again he stopped and put a tiny stone into his pocket. There were one or two walkers about, some coming from the cliff path further up the shore. Some children stopped to watch him but were too shy to ask him what he was doing. It was then he'd had the strangest feeling that he was being watched, not by the children, they'd gone. He glanced up and twisted his head around to look over his shoulder. There, not an arm's reach away was the girl.

'Oh. Hello,' he started.

She didn't answer. She dropped her head and her dark hair fell about her shoulders and the collar of a faintly patterned blouse with long sleeves. She looked at him intently for what seemed minutes. Michael brushed his hands on his trousers and struggled to get up. At least he now knew she was real. He was about to open his mouth to speak to her when he realised she'd gone. Like yesterday, there was nowhere she could have gone to. She'd simply vanished.

Michael's credulity had now been challenged to its limits. There was no way he could lever the experience into his philosophy or, on the other hand, ignore it. It was his problem and until he could find some kind of rational explanation for it he thought that he'd better keep it to himself. A part of him wanted to forget what had happened but a larger part of him hoped that the illusion, if it was some kind of illusion, would return for he had to admit that he'd found the young lady devastatingly attractive. In short, he'd like to see her again.

THE
HOTEL

CHAPTER SIX

Dick and Annie soon warmed up in the cosy front bar of the Bay Hotel. There were several others there including a couple who had just completed the coast to coast walk.

'Feel a bit guilty at leaving your mother to do all the work,' said Dick.

'You look it, with a pint in your hand,' returned Annie.

'Seriously, we ought to be getting back soon.'

'I think she's glad to have you out from under her feet for a bit. What time do you normally have dinner?'

'About six usually.'

'Well, we've half an hour yet. Tell me some more about the chap we've just seen outside.'

'Michael? Well he's been coming here for almost as long as we have. It must have been the early sixties when I got to know him better. He's a lecturer at Oxford and quite well thought of. Written a couple of books which were talked about at the time though I don't think he's done anything lately. He must be about retirement age or going on that way.'

'Do you know how long he's been dowsing?'

'Oh, for ages. We used to tease him at first when we saw him about the village with a forked twig. We stopped when he found a missing gold ring which was reported lost between Bridge End and Fisherhead.'

'Do you know if he dowses for anything else besides missing objects?'

'I think he helped to trace the water pipes to a cottage at the end of Sunnyside once and then there was the matter of helping to find a missing child who hadn't come up from the beach. Turned out that the lad had broken his foot badly trying to climb out of a scaur run, jammed it into a crack in the rock and fallen awkwardly. He'd hopped and crawled out of danger but was in too much pain to continue up the beach and so lay there waiting for someone to find him. It was Michael who drew a quick sketch of the beach, waved a pencil over it and said, "You'll find him there," and they did.'

'That's map dowsing,' said Annie. 'We do that sometimes.'

'It's all a mystery to me. Drink up, we'd better be on our way.'

Dick, Sylvia and Annie enjoyed a splendid dinner washed down with an excellent bottle of South African Cabernet Sauvignon. The conversation flowed warmly from family doings and interests to arrangements for Christmas leaving them all glad to be together if only for a few days. As it darkened outside, the wind lived up to its earlier promise and strengthened from the north east. Few folk were seen passing the window and when Dick rose to pull the curtains the street was empty. He could hear a boisterous sea as it shoaled and steepened over the uneven ground and could imagine the scene shortly as it would obscure the windows and slam impetuously up the slip in a confusion of explosive glee. He half listened for any other noises but couldn't catch anything. Returning to the extended gate-legged table he smiled and resumed his seat. Sylvia and Annie were still talking quietly and Pam's last letter was on the table. It had been one of those intimate, open family occasions when all present felt in touch with each other's worlds. Annie seemed animated and confident and he felt pleased that she appeared to have put her problems behind her. They shared the clearing up and put a match to the fire. There remained only a choice of music, television or more conversation. Dick felt that the first two were destined to be overlaid by the third and so switched on his tape player for a favourite classical background accompaniment to their widening topics. By eleven o' clock Annie was beginning to feel tired and making her excuses, she went up. Within a minute or two Sylvia had followed leaving Dick to switch everything off and lock up.

Dick was tired too, his two excursions had been enjoyable but had left him feeling pleasantly relaxed. He took up the poker and scraped the fire together and settled for a while to review the day.

A loud grunt opposite him brought him up with a start. A smallish man with wisps of white hair surrounding a sun-darkened complexion sat opposite him. He was grinning hugely and his eyes twinkled with amusement. He was dressed in a baggy blue gansey and a pair of faded canvas trousers that finished tightly at the knee. Long woollen socks were rolled down around his calves above a pair of stout leather boots. His hands, that were resting on his thighs, were scarred and bent with domed and clawlike nails. He nodded slowly.

'Ye can see me at last. I bin tryin' for years to get through. Stand a watch alongside me. I got somethin' to share wi' 'ee!'
Dick felt somehow more prepared for this than he had been. He had Annie to thank for that but it was, nevertheless, an incredible experience. Here he was sitting at his own fireside looking at someone who couldn't be there. The figure shuffled closer to the fire and peered across the short distance that separated them.

'I tried everythin', even sang shanties to 'ee but ye didn't take a blind bit o' notice. I thought ye'd be like all the rest, put it down to 'magination or sheer off in a frit. I blame the Reformation for it. They threw overboard the idea of souls in the doldrums, straight to 'eaven or 'ell they said, overturnin' centuries of concern for the poor buggers who'd died. No masses for us, no bother about our souls at all. God's dogs, they were a tight arsed crew! You lot aren't any better. Your narrow-beamed beliefs don't let us aboard. Now, cousin, you'm a sailor, sit this watch out with me 'cos I got somethin' to say to 'ee.'

'Like you, I 'ad several ships but the ones that was close to my 'eart was the old *Unity* an' the *Wrath of God*. Most of my story I can tell for myself but the bit when I was shifted into the *Wrath* I 'ad to borrow from my shipmates. You'll see why.'

Dick sat back and locked his fingers on his lap. The voice was from the west with heavily accented vowels, easy on the ear but sometimes a bit fast for him.

'My name is Andrew Talbot an' I were sailin' master's mate of the pinnace *Unity* of Exeter out of Topsam. This were a couple of years before the sailin' of the "felicissima invencible" fleet against England which you'll remember were 'arried up the Channel by war and by weather to be wrecked all around our coasts. Twelve weeks after we'd sailed, the old *Unity* in company with the *Grace* under young Walter Ednay, were returnin' from the east coast of Central Americee when we fell in with a Spanish galleon. This great grey shape moved up against us in the mornin' watch. We must 'ave been 'alf asleep! The *Grace* were 'ull down fine on the larboard bow. I were on watch, piped all 'ands but it were no good. The Spanish vessel were closed up for action an' within minutes a wicked storm o' lead an' iron 'ad swept the decks bringin' 'avoc as the crew tried to bring the guns to bear. The ragged broadside that followed tore the backstays out o' the starboard side an' we lost our main topmast. By now the crew 'ad lost their nerve. A lot of 'em jumped overboard. There were precious little opposition to the boarding party of Spanish soldiers.'

'I was aft alongside the Master and the Cap'n with three of our crew but it were 'opeless. The Spanish beat us back to the quarter rail, one of our lads was shot an' went over the side an' the Cap'n fell wounded in the chest and leg. The Bosun and I fought side by side an' the goin' were gettin' tougher. I remember the sweat runnin' down into my eyes and my arm getting so tired I could 'ardly lift it. We stuck one or two of 'em but there were always another bugger be'ind 'im waiting to have a go. When we couldn't go on any longer we gave in and expected to be killed but some officer or other shouted out an' we was shoved aboard the Spaniard to the cheers of her crew.

She were the *Santa Anna* of Cadiz, a bloody great ship wi' four masts an' swarmin' with soldiers.'

The old chap had become quite animated and was using his hands to great effect. Dick could almost see the fight that had taken place and had leaned forward in his chair.

'I were dragged below, shackled, an' shoved with my companions into a cable or cordage store somewhere aft an' below the waterline. Muffled gunfire followed an' we guessed the fate of the poor *Unity*. 'Twere then that the Master told us he'd been wounded in the side but there were nothing we could do for 'im. As our eyes became used to the dark we squared ourselves up as best we could, 'uddled up in a corner an' waited for morning. Nobody slept, nobody spoke. We were too dazed an' tired. Only a matter of hours ago we were sailing along safely. It were the Bosun I remember who spoke first.

" 'As anyone got a knife or spike?"

Strangely enough, the Spanish soldiers 'adn't searched us when they chained us up an' although our wrists an' ankles were manacled, we found that we still 'ad a knife an' a marlin spike between us. Jus' then, the door was flung open an' a couple of Spanish soldiers come in. One 'ad a lanthorn an' the other 'ad a drawn sword. We thought our time was up! Then the bigger of the two 'it me with the flat of 'is sword an' pulled me up.

"You," he screams. "Up!"

I remember feeling the blood comin' down through me eyebrows an' tryin' to clear it away with me 'ands bolted together. The soldier kept proddin' me with 'is sword. I dragged myself up the steep ladders an' out on the well deck in the brilliant morning sunshine. I were pushed up the ladder aft to the quarter deck where the Commodore stood with 'is officers. The Cap'n spoke to me in English.

"You are now prisoners of His Majesty. Are you the Captain of the *Unity*?"

I were thinkin' of how to answer this when the soldier 'it me again with the flat of 'is sword. O my God, the bloody deck spun round an' I could hardly stand up.

"You are Captain of the *Unity* I understand."

"No. I..., I'm the Mate."

"We are bound to a South American port. When we return you and your friends will go to the galleys."

He turned to the guard.

"Take him below."

I were pushed roughly below. The door were opened and I were flung in. Breakfast was waitin'. A few biscuits an' a stone jug of water. Bosun says,

"We shan't starve then."

"We shan't get very fat either," says the lad.

I told them we were three decks down, almost under the steering gallery itself. We settled down to a long day.

Days passed during which we was fed each mornin' with a double handful of oatmeal biscuits an' a jug of water. We was not allowed out of our prison or given any help for the wounded man. Our wrists an' ankles became very sore with the chafin' of the rough steel an' the scabs that formed soon became infected and swollen.'

Andrew thrust his hands out and looked up into Dick's face with a pugnacious air.

'It were during the third week that we 'eard a workin' party in the compartment next door. I've got a fair understandin' of Spanish so I pressed my ear against the boardin' to see if I could catch anythin' A bit later I heard two pieces of important information. They was bound out to rendezvous with a treasure ship an' escort it back to Spain an' they were being shadowed by a largish vessel without any identification. Not that they seemed disturbed by this news. They was well able to take care of themselves. I passed this on to my friends.'

'As the days passed, we put the marline spike to good use an' everyone spent an hour or two on their chains. A sharp tug would part 'em. The clasp an' lock on me wrist cuffs were almost broken an' a 'eavy knock would do the trick. We also worked on the door 'inges so that a good kickin' would bring it down Of course we didn't know if there would ever be the opportunity to do anythin' about it but it did us good to be doin' somethin'.'

'We jus' waited an' prayed an' hoped that something would 'appen to give us a chance to get the 'ell out.'

'Four weeks after the sinking of the *Unity* we was still quartered in the cordage store. The Master were now very weak an' 'is wound looked terrible. He never complained an' stayed cheerful despite the fact that he must 'ave been in a lot of pain. 'Twas either a Monday or a Tuesday evenin' in the fourth week when we 'eard a commotion above. Men were runnin' to and fro. The rumble of 'eavy guns bein' run to be loaded an' primed. Shouted orders an' the squeal of blocks vied with each other as the boats was loaded an' swung over the side as was the custom in battle. This cleared the decks for action an' made sure that the boats was not shot full of 'oles.'

Dick butted in.

'Used to take us just over three minutes to close up gun crews on the corvette but then we only had a four-inch, a pom-pom, a couple of machine guns and, of course, the depth charges.'

Andrew continued.

'We was certain that the Spanish vessel were preparin' to engage. A wild plan flashed through my mind. In the mayhem followin' the first broadside from the enemy vessel, we'd kick down the door, get up on deck an' climb down the boat-rope to the boats being towed behind. It was bloody stupid but it was all we 'ad. So, with all agreein' we parted our chains an' waited. A silence fell over the vessel. Then an ear shatterin' crash shook the very frames as fifteen or more iron balls drove into 'er at close range. As the Dons answered fire, we kicked the door down an' the four of us, pale, dirty an' tremblin' crep out of the store an' made our way on deck. Dense clouds of smoke, confusion, noise, shouts and screams met us but nobody seemed to notice us as we ran doubled up to the side opposite the action. The Bosun helped the Master over the side an' lashed him to the boat-rope. The AB an' I crouched under the bulwarks. Still nobody noticed us there! Another broadside crashed into the Spanish craft. Foot long splinters flew through the air an' flames started to run up the mains'l. A hail of lead thudded into the masts an' bulwarks. A great groove of white wood appeared right close to my 'ead. We took our chance an' leaped onto the cappin' an' swung, 'and over 'and down the boat-rope. The Master was just 'auling 'imself into the boat and the Bosun were 'elping him inboard. We reached the boat, shakin' like babies an' started to slash an' cut through the boat-rope with the seaman's hand-knife. Of course it were then that we was spotted. Bullets spattered about us as we sawed at the 'eavy rope. Several bullets 'it the boat while some enterprisin' soldier started to haul the rope in. Then sudden like, the rope parted an' we fell astern of 'er. God's blood, that were a close thing!'

'On droppin' astern we could see the vessel that 'ad attacked us. She weren't flyin' any colours but by 'er lines, she looked an English-built vessel. She were longer an' lower than the Spaniard which was why she had come in close. The Spaniard would have difficulty in bringin' 'er guns to bear on a target lower than 'erself while the lower vessel could do terrible damage about the waterline. We began to signal the attacker 'cos this were our only hope of rescue. Meanwhile, we started to search the boat for any provisions or useful items. We turned up a cask of water, another of biscuit and a packet of dried fish. The small chests of ornate clothin', bundles an' furniture, we slung over the side.'

'The further we drifted astern, the lower our chances were of bein' picked up by the attackin' vessel. I went over to the Master who was lyin' in the bows. 'E looked very ill an' the movement 'adn't done 'im any good at all. Two cables ahead of us the battle were still goin' on an' smoke were beginnin' to hide both craft. The second part of the plan were not goin' well.'

'As dusk grew slowly into night we worked out a rough estimate of our position from the stars. Surprisingly enough, we found we was only a matter of a degree or so from the position we 'ad been attacked in. It became clear to me that the Spaniard must be cruisin' in this region for good reason. Then I remembered the conversation I'd overheard about her bein' bound out to act as an escort to a treasure ship. This, coupled with the fact that she'd engaged two other vessels in the area, convinced me that the rendezvous would be in this very area an' probably soon.'

'There were no bloody oars in the boat an' so there was nought we could do about the boat's course as it drifted away into the night. Later we wished we 'adn't thrown the clothing over the side 'cos it got quite cold. When dawn come we found ourselves alone. Nothing in sight at all. The Master lay very still an' we thought 'e'd become senseless. We agreed to limit the water to 'alf a pint a day an' the biscuits to a handful a day as we'd been used to but we weren't very confident about the future.'

'As you know, Caribbean is a 'uge sea and the sailin' lines through it, though well enough used, are few and far between. It grew warmer as the sun rose an' it promised to be a scorcher. Bosun were concerned about the Master an' wondered if 'e could make 'im more comfortable. 'E took off 'is shirt an' rolled it up an' put it under the older man's 'ead. Master's breathing 'ad become irregular and 'is wound 'ad started to bleed again, the dull red blood seepin' over the brown crusty stains of the previous weeks. I thought it amazin' that 'e'd managed to last as long as 'e 'ad. 'E were a lovely man and I'd been with 'im for a number of trips. The day dragged by under a burnin', blazin' sun we 'ad never reckoned with aboard ship. It seemed so much 'otter to us having spent weeks in semi-darkness. The Bosun was forced to retrieve 'is shirt. As 'e did so the Master 'alf rose to a sittin' position an' made as if to speak, then fell back, 'is eyes starin' straight before 'im, quite dead.

" 'E's gone then," says Bosun.

"To a better place that this," declares the AB. " 'E were a fine man. Will you say somethin' for 'im?"

The Bosun stared fixedly over the side an' the sailor made the sign of the cross.

"Receive thy servant, our friend, O Lord." I said. " An' take 'im to thyself on the day when the sea shall give up 'er dead. Amen."

"Amen," repeated the two of them.

"We'd better get 'im over the side," says Bosun.

It were only then that we discovered how weak we'd become. The efforts of the previous day 'ad taken every last ounce of strength 'cos try as 'ard as we could, we couldn't lift 'im over the side. The Master 'ad not been a small man an' the last weeks 'ad not robbed 'im of a great deal of weight.

"We'll 'ave to leave 'im."

"In this 'eat?"

"Nought else we can do."

"Perhaps we'll be picked up soon."

"Perhaps," I said, but I were beginning to think otherwise. The hours passed and burned into night. leaving us exhausted an' 'opeless. Days blazed across the brassy sky an' there was no pause in the relentless gaze of the blisterin' sun. Within the week the fresh water give out. On the ninth day the seaman died. Nobody noticed when 'e went. 'E just weren't alive any more.'

Dick looked concerned.

'We picked up boats in the Atlantic on more than one occasion. The poor devils were often in a bad way, if alive at all. Go on.'

'More days blazed agonizingly by. It became 'ard to tell just when I were awake. Much later I noticed that the Bosun 'ad gone. I lacked the strength or will to do anything. Life became a fantasy of dancin', scaldin' light. Pain, heat an' light swam over me in waves. Often I found myself back in the fields an' cool woods of my childhood. I were runnin', laughin' with my brother goin' down to the pool below the waterfall. I'd plunge into the green deep an' then twist toward the light on the surface above me.'

'Then I'd burst into consciousness an' the pain beat about my 'ead once more. Yellow, orange light lanced into my eyes but I were too weak to look away. I were faintly aware of the others though I could no longer place how they 'ad come there. Something did not smell good but I couldn't place that either. Dream an' heat, heat an' pain closed into a merciful darkness.'

'Then I become aware of movement. Someone or somethin' was movin' me upwards. I thought I must be dyin'. Next I felt cooler and began to understand that there were folk near me, helpin' me, talkin' to me. I tried to move, tried to speak but it all seemed too far away, yet somehow I felt safer an' dropped into a deep sleep.'

Andrew's voice dropped almost to a whisper. His face had become taut and his mouth tight lipped. He fell silent for a while and stared long into the fire. Dick took a deep breath and would have reached out to touch the old man encouragingly but wasn't sure if he could or ought. Instead, he poked at the fire and put a couple of small logs on the back.

'There,' sighed Andrew, 'I haven't spat that out for centuries.'

'I know something of the shock and fear of action at sea,' returned Dick, still wishing somehow that he could show his feelings at such a tale.

'We ferried the wounded back from the Normandy beaches in 1944. I know how grateful many of the poor chaps felt as we took them aboard.'

'That's only the start of my story, as you've probably guessed, we was spotted by a friendly ship an' I were 'auled aboard.'

CHAPTER SEVEN

'My rescue ship were *The Wrath of God* eight weeks out of Bristol with a cargo of cannon balls an' casks of black powder. She were Bristol built in 1580. Only last year she'd been thoroughly overhauled, careened, re-rigged an' fitted out with a new fore-topmast an' main top-gallant mast. She carried a full set of spare spars an' enough elm planking for Chips to rebuild her bulwarks completely. Enough cordage were stored below to re-rig 'er twice over. She were launched from the yard of Charles Watson on the Redcliffe side of the river as the *Samuel.* Nothing but the best estate grown English oak an' elm had been used in 'er construction. She were a beautiful graceful craft, quite large for 'er year, being some hundred odd feet long with a beam of twenty five foot. Er prowess lay in 'er speed of sailing. With some slight adjustments to the weight fore an' aft she'd make a knot or two more than most other vessels of 'er size an' tonnage.'

'She carried thirty guns, twelve to larboard an' twelve to starboard. She mounted three swivels in the bow an' two aft while lashed amidships was the great gun, captured from a central American port in '61, an' the only relic of the skipper's previous command.'

'The present crew 'ad been together for some four an' a half years an' were as well knit an' seasoned a group of rascals as could be found in a day's sailing. After a week or two I got to know an' respect them. The Cap'n were one Martin Skellworthy from Hotwells an' the Master were Amos Pollard from Porlock. Pollard were 'is real name but Skellworthy were a borrowed name to suit the times. Amos 'ad been at sea for over thirty five years an' 'ad so many adventures 'e almost never spoke about them unless with a wry touch of humour an' a smile. 'E were a little, bent old man thatched with little wisps of white hair across a bronzed head. 'Is 'ands was the 'ands of the mariner, gnarled, bent an' amazin' strong. There were very little about sailing ships that old Amos didn't know. E'd sailed them all, from the slow heavy warships of the present Queen's father, whoops! you know who I mean, to the fast Revenue cruisers in the service of Queen Mary which were largely why 'e were in the West Indies an' not diggin' a bean patch somewhere in England. Elizabeth weren't keen on such as served Queen Mary!'

'There were Lofty, Chess, Gukho an' Chips, Farmer, Barbados an' the Gentleman. There were Monk an' Silent, Diabalo an' Dancer, William, the Frenchman an' young Hoppin' Jack. From surgeon to swordsman, from Bosun to Shantyman, each were a master at 'is craft an' though their differences were 'uge their ability to respect each other's talents were greater than their tempers. My oppo' were Thomas Gridley. 'E were a 'ard man. Griddo to the crew but never to 'is face. P'raps 'e drove the men too hard but 'e 'ad their respect in a tight corner. 'E were a dedicated swordsman, tall, lean an' agile. They all 'ad dreams, dreams of riches, dreams of silver an' gold, dreams of 'and to 'and fightin' with the 'ated Don an' a last great dream of all, to sail in triumph up the River Avon, loaded to the gunwales with treasure from the mines of the Americas.'

'John Craftesman, Master Gunner, prayed nightly grinnin' to 'imself, "Oh Lord, send us a fair wind an' a fat Spaniard!" They all knew the need for discipline for although the ship were a model of efficiency, trim an' shipshape, the skipper wanted a well-run ship an' a task for each an' every hour of the day. 'Oly-stoning for the mornin' watch, scrapin' and varnishin' during the forenoon, ropework in the afternoon an' washin' down in the Dogs. Then came the thousand an' one tasks that made the *Wrath* a first rate fightin' unit. Weapons to clean an' lay to readiness. Gun carriages to oil an' check. Tackles to overhaul an' cordage to replace. Lashin's to check and whippin's to renew.'

'Of great importance were the weapons, always kept clean an' bright. Pistols to be cleaned, loaded an' primed. Pikes to be burnished an' lashed in racks on the upper deck. Cutlasses 'oned to a razor's edge. The naval system of watches were worked on board as were the standards of gunnery. Ol' John, the Master Gunner, apart from a 'uge sense of 'umour, just 'appened to be an ex-Master Gunner in the navy of Henry VIII. 'E knew the mysteries of range, elevation an' recoil an' 'ow to get the best from 'is brood of thirty noisy children, as 'e called 'em.'

'There were two armouries on board the *Wrath,* one for'ard an' one aft. This were in case the vessel were boarded an' the crew split up. Then there'd be an ample supply of weapons at 'and for both parties. Apart from the vessels armament an' the boardin' weapons, each crew member 'ad 'is own brace of pistols, cutlass and knife. Some, like Diabalo, went for a fancy curved sword of Arabian steel while Gentleman boasted a fine brace of silver inlaid wheel-lock pistols with ivory 'andles.'

'The quartermaster's mate, Jason, were another tall man of about thirty five years. 'E'd been at sea since 'e were a lad an' were the only survivor of the *ffaulcon*, wrecked off Port Royal in the seventies. 'E'd spent three years on the plantations an' were self-conscious about the lash scars on 'is face 'an chest. 'E wore a red buttoned-up shirt an' a red neckerchief to 'ide these marks. Unlike the mate, Jason were a savage fighter, entirely lackin' in skill an' precision. 'Owever 'e amply made up for this by 'is remembrance of three years as a guest of the Spanish. To watch 'is bitterness with a cutlass was not pleasant.'

'Silent were a mystery. Nobody knew where 'e came from an' nobody 'ad never 'eard 'im speak. 'E were a fierce fighter, a good man to have by one's side in trouble an' an extremely able sailor. In common with Lofty, 'e could throw a knife the breadth of the ship with accuracy an' was a member of the quarterdeck party in times of action. Silent's 'atred of the Spanish were indicated by the narrowin' of 'is eyes when 'e 'eard mention of the Dons. 'E seldom smiled an' were as different from Barbados as two men could be. Barbados always smiled. 'E too came from the plantations. An excellent swimmer, 'twere rumoured 'e joined 'is first ship by swimmin' five miles out after escapin' from the plantations. Before joinin' this crew 'e'd never 'andled a cutlass but now 'e were as formidable as the mate 'isself.'

Dick smiled. 'You get to know your shipmates when there's dozens of you all sharing the same small space.'

'After I were picked up, it took me a few days to come to myself. Couldn' go up on deck without help or without coverin' up. When I were a bit more steady an' feelin' better I'd go up on my own an' 'ave a yarn with Amos. In the evenin's we'd listen to Dancer. 'E used to sit cross-legged on the capstan 'ead like a little tailor an' fiddle away to 'is 'eart's delight. It were Dancer who made light of much of the 'eavy work aboard wi' 'is cheerful shanties an' songs. 'E were the soul an' spirit of the *Wrath* wi' 'is music an' songs. Thomas used to say that to 'ave Dancer aboard was not to worry what the cook was like. Nobody were ever miserable long in the 'earin' of they cheerful songs that filled the vessel after sundown. I sang 'ee some, remember?'

Dick nodded and realised why he'd found the notes oddly familiar. Sea shanties weren't heard much on board ship in his day but they could be heard in pubs and on the stage. He knew a few. He looked across at Andrew who was smiling and nodding as he talked. He had the habit of raising his finger level with his eye to emphasise a point and Dick found him a strong and interesting character to listen to.

'Well, with a few good meals inside me an' plenty of rest I soon found my feet an' became a seaman on board. Of course I told old Amos all about the treasure ship an' 'e told the skipper so I weren't surprised when Cap'n Martin found me on the forenoon an' said, "I'll 'ave that position you spoke of." 'E went on to ask me about the fightin' prowess of the *Santa Anna* an' 'ow big she were. I told 'im 'ow when we escaped she'd been engaged in an action starboard side to with a long, lean black-painted vessel that flew no colours. I mentioned the damage done but couldn't say what 'appened in the end. The Cap'n brought a chart up an' we marked off the position as best could. Then 'e says, "With a bit of luck, we'll avenge the death of your friends an' sail home rich as kings." Then 'e added, " Reckon I know your long, lean vessel. I've seen 'er before, nearer home than this. She'd be the *Reformation* of Watchet. Like this vessel she carries a pretty tough crew dedicated to fighting the Don." '

'The Cap'n soon became convinced that the *Santa Anna* were a vessel sent out to guard the same ship 'e were after. 'E were further convinced that this ship were fairly close and probably bound for the Windward Passage. The position I'd given 'im confirmed this. Next, 'e called all the officers an' fuglemen aft an' asked me to tell my story. I left nought out.'

'Then Cap'n 'e says, "From what we've 'eard we can safely conclude that the *Santa Anna* were sent out to escort the vessel we're after. We know that she were in two recent engagements. In the first we learn of 'er strength an' in the second we 'ave evidence that she received three broadsides low on the starboard side. Both these actions took place within five weeks an' within twenty mile of each other so the escort is cruising in a region which Andrew Talbot an' I 'ave agreed to be about sixty mile to the sou-sou-west of our present position. Dependin' on the damage done by our friend Cap'n Perkins of the *Reformation*, which, if I know Cap'n

Perkins, will be quite considerable, we shouldn't find the teave too 'ot." '

' "Now," says skipper. "We 'ave two courses open to us. Either we can cruise 'ere in the Bight of Leogane an' chevy 'em when they 'ove in sight or we can mark off a course from the Passage to the meetin' place an' sail to meet 'em. They'll be looking for trouble in the Passage but they'll not be expectin' it miles out in the Caribbean. Well gentlemen, I put it to you. What shall we do?" '

'I remember lookin' round. All eyes were on the Cap'n an' then John Craftesman spoke up.

"My children are ready an' we've powder a'plenty. We sail."

"Aye!" joined in Thomas, Jason an' the others.

"We sail! We sail!"

"Very good, pass the word, we sail in the demi-hour by my glass. Double up runnin' riggin' on the main an' tops'l yards. Lay up shot on deck an' check all carriages. Break open a cask of spirit an' issue a nipperkin all round. I want this ship closed up for action an' standin' by at eight bells. Carry on please." '

'The meetin' broke up with a sense of purpose. Each man went swiftly about 'is particular job until all were silent at their posts. I could see that this vessel would never be caught nappin' as we'd been. Thomas strode the upper deck, a wary eye open for anythin' out-o-place.

"All's well Cap'n."

"Very good," says Cap'n Martin, an' eight bells rang out from for'ard.

"Master Gridley!" says Cap'n. "Run up our colours an' we'll throw some fear into these 'ontish Spanish. God blind me if we don't."

Thomas went below to his cabin an' shortly a dark bundle was seen to move in a series of jerks to the mainmast truck. A quiet tug an' a grinnin' death 'ead floated away against the welkin'. The *Wrath* were lookin' for trouble.'

Dick thought of the dozens of times when the crew of the corvette had closed up for action or when he'd been on the beaches ready to open up with everything the LST had. The old man had his interest now and he felt that he was right there alongside him in the *Wrath*.

Andrew paused and licked his lips.

'I could do with a tankard o' swipes,' he grinned.

'When the vessel were closed up for action,' he continued, 'both watches carried on as usual but the craftsmen an' fuglemen stood-to in two watches. When All-Hands were called everyone who wasn't actually doin' somethin' turned out on deck. Down below the galley fire were put out an' Chess prepared 'is instruments. Chess were the surgeon an' many a lad were grateful 'e were aboard. Did I say 'ow 'e got 'is name? Well, the 'andles of a surgeon's knife 'ad 'andles of boxwood an' boxwood is the wood that most chess sets are made of. If you could 'ave a peep inside Chess's sea bag you'd see a beautiful set of intricate carved boxwood chessmen which come on board as the 'andles of 'is tools!'

'As the *Wrath* moved purposeful out into the Caribbean with all 'ands standin' by, only thirty mile ahead of 'er the *San Pedro di Puerto de Santa Maria* an' the *Santa Anna* moved slowly to meet us. The *Santa Anna* was somewhat low by the bow largely due to damage done by a score or so of spherical iron balls manufactured in Bristol an' transported to the Caribbean on board the *Reformation* of Watchet. It didn't 'ave a very encouragin' effect on the crew. The *San Pedro* was commanded by Juan Felipe Fernandez, a short, dark, serious man with many years at sea. The serious bit was due to 'im signing a cargo book for several ton of gold, silver an' precious stones from the mines of the Andes an' bound for the treasury of Spain. 'E was sincerely 'opin' that 'e would be allowed to fulfil 'is commission. The *San Pedro* were not a fighting ship. She were reasonable armed an' manned an' carried a contingent of soldiers but without a good escort she felt a mite vulnerable.'

'You've got to remember Dick, that in those days a sea voyage were a very perilous affair. Unless you 'ad guns pokin' out of every 'ole in the bulwarks you could count on bein' stopped by some bugger or 'nother bigger an' better armed than you. Merchant ships were fair game for the Turks, the Dutch, the Frenchies an' Algerian pirates apart from the Dons. You could easily end up as a Musselman's slave or chained to an oar while on a trip from Bristol to Plymouth. God's dogs, the buggers were everywhere.'

Dick thought back to the war. At least he knew who he was fighting.

'Just after six bells in the forenoon, the lookout, 'igh on the *Wrath*'s main t'gallant yard, hailed the deck.

"Deck ho!"

"What do you see?"

"Two sailing vessels dead ahead!"
"Very good," answers Thomas an' turns to the Cap'n.
"Two sailing vessels dead ahead Cap'n."
Cap'n Martin smiled without showin' 'is teeth. "Then we are in time. They've got to be the *Anna* an' the treasure galleon. Order the 'ands to look to their weapons. Double up on the staff there Quartermaster! All 'ands to stand to!"
The order was carried for'ard.
"All hands!"

At once the decks of the *Wrath* were alive with sailors making the final preparations for action. All 'er guns were loaded, primed an' run out. Slow matches were lit an' powder put by under damp cloth with the guidance of John Craftesman. The gun crews were tyin' squares of kerseymere about their 'eads an' knottin' neckerchiefs about their throats not for any fashionable reasons but to protect 'emselves against the noise, fumes an' smoke from the iron monsters under their charge. The big gun were loaded with a cask of small bullets, about five centuries of 'em, an' John reckoned that this, fired through the stern windows from dead astern or fired low across the deck, would just about finish the 'ardest enemy. As the big gun was brought to bear over the starboard gunwhale an' chocked an' lashed into position, Amos 'ad the boats lowered on the burtons down into the 'old. Amos reckoned that it made the ship just that bit more manoeuvrable an' further, the crew would fight better with their only means of escape below their feet an' not bobbin' about a few yards astern.'

'As the vessels come into clear view I recognised the bigger one alright an' called out. The Cap'n nodded.

"Target fine on the starboard bow, range, one mile!" shouted the Gunner's Mate.

As we come up on them, the *Anna* was cruisin' to larboard of the treasure ship thus leaving 'er charge open to attack. Unless she dropped astern an' made up in between the *Wrath* an' the bullion ship, she'd not be able to bring 'er guns into action for fear of hittin' the *Pedro*. It were a beautiful play an' not one you'd expect to find. As the distance grew less, the way fell off the Spanish vessels as they decided what course of action to follow. They were two to one but they couldn't afford to ignore a vessel under our colours. The breeze were now light an' the two of them were making about two or three knots. We were a good three cables to windward. To keep this favourable position we put our main yards aback an' 'ove to. The next move was the Don's.'

'On 'er present course, the *Anna* would show 'er shot-damaged side. 'Owever, she 'ad no time to draw ahead, go about an' come back at us with 'er undamaged side. Cap'n Martin stood by the starboard rail with a skri-glass to 'is eye. It were Italian an' quite a rare piece. 'E used to say that soon every ship would possess such a instrument. The two Spanish ships now lay still. Then the *Anna*'s yards were braced around an' she slowly swung astern of the *Pedro* an' took up a position on 'er larboard quarter.'

'Now was the time for battle. The *Pedro* were now part covered by the mass of the *Anna*. Once the *Anna* 'ad been dealt with, the galleon lay unprotected. What was greatly in our favour was that the *Anna* showed us 'er action-damaged side. John Craftesman's 'unch 'ad proved to be right when 'e positioned the big gun to starboard but thinkin' about it, I reckon 'e knew which way the wind was blowin' in more ways than one!

The Cap'n turned to the Sailing Master an' Master Gunner.

"Amos," 'e said quietly, "I want 'er brought up 'alf a cables length from the *Anna*. I intend to engage 'er an' try to sink 'er, then pass under 'er stern an' attack the treasure ship on the larboard side. Save the big gun for passin' under the stern or, if things get difficult, after we've engaged the main target."

Both men nodded an' went to their stations.

Slowly at first, an' then more swiftly, the *Wrath of God* slid through the water. We could see the soldiers millin' about on deck. Burnished steel gleamed in the late afternoon sun as their 'elmets an' breast-plates reflected the lowerin' rays.

The gun crews stood silent, waitin'.'

'As the *Wrath* swam into 'er 'pointed position, John Craftesman 'eld up 'is 'and. The crews watched 'im. 'Is 'and flashed down!

"Fire!" 'e screamed.

The *Wrath* rocked with the recoil as twelve guns belched jagged tongues of flame. Acrid smoke cleared away toward the Spaniard. It were just the way Old John liked it. The smoke from both vessels would lay back aboard the enemy. Screams an' cries told us our shots 'ad gone 'ome. Back come the guns, swabbed, loaded, primed an' rolled out, their iron muzzles starin' from the side. As each crew finished the exercise they glanced up at the Master Gunner, each gun's cap'n holdin' up an 'and.

"Small wedges!" shouted John, 'is 'and ready to give the next signal. Each crew drove 'ome the smallest of the set of wedges provided to elevate or depress the guns. 'Ands rose again in unison.

"Fire!"

Again the guns crashed, straining against their tackles. This time, lances of flame darted from the Spaniard's side an' the whine of flyin' iron was 'eard as the balls from a ragged-arse broadside tore over'ead. Some balls struck the *Wrath* topside, but no yards or riggin' fell to the deck thanks to the order to double up the runnin' riggin' an' only a few splinters showered down.'

A strong gust of wind squalled up King Street, setting the windows rattling and the coats to sway on the back of the door. Dick bent forward and pushed the fire together, putting the last log firmly in the centre. Andrew leaned back in his chair and ran his fingers through his sparse hair as he looked ruefully around the little parlour.

'Asn't changed much. Still got wind an' water comin' inboard.'

He went on. 'The wind was bringin' us in closer. The enemy swivel guns come into action, independent, an' the first casualties were received aboard the *Wrath*. One of the larboard gun's crew were thrown 'eavily against the bulwarks by a ball which drove on through the unfortunate sailor an' through the elm plankin' leavin' a brilliant splash on the yellow deckin'. Young Jack, on a signal from the Master Gunner, drew up a bucket of water an' swilled the blood into the scuppers. John didn't reckon blood cheered the crew, special if it were left lyin' around at the start of an action. Later, there would probably be a lot more an' no time to wash it down. The body lay face upwards, limp in the scuppers, a look of surprise across its face. It were William, an old 'and an' a kindly man.'

'With the use of wedges the second broadside 'ad been brought lower an' a ragged cheer went up from our crew as the smoke cleared an' we could see the splintered gashes in the *Anna*'s side. The Spaniard continued a wicked random fire from 'er falconets, murderers an' top-pieces. With 'er large crew she could employ the extra 'ands to work these weapons. Bullets an' shot spattered us but no major damage was so far evident.'

'By this time we was abaft the Don's quarter an' the Quartermasters were preparin' to turn an' pass astern of 'er. The Master Gunner's 'and swept down again.

"Fire!"

This time the flying iron wrought 'avoc about 'er stern, splinterin' the finely carved woodwork an' shatterin' the patternwork about the after gunports. Several soldiers were seen to drop. Then the blows began to fall in earnest. The second Spanish broadside were more effective than the first. One gun were overturned an' the crew flung sprawlin' an' 'urt across the deck. A jagged 'ole 'ad appeared in the quarterdeck plankin' where a ball 'ad driven through at deck level. '

'Smoke, confusion, yells, blood an' sweat on a late 'ot summer's afternoon an' calmly John Craftesman's 'and went up, an' down! Again, up an' down! Barbados, 'is eyes tight shut, clutched 'is thigh where a gurt wooden splinter 'ad driven through just above 'is knee. Thomas's face was streamin' blood! Jason gritted 'is teeth, one 'and on the staff, t'other 'angin' useless by 'is side, drippin' steady into a growin' pool on the deck.

'Skipper now signalled Amos to take the vessel astern of the *Anna* as planned. She moved slowly out the sights of the Don's large guns and presented 'er entire length to the stern of the *Anna*. Gradual, the big gun itself come opposite the stern windows.

"John!" indicated the Captain.

John was already ahead.

"Fire!"

The entire stern section of the Spaniard became a twisted shambles of matchwood as five century of lead shot tore through at point blank range.'

'Shock, then terror prevailed on the *Anna*'s decks as man after man tumbled into a bloody 'eap, their fine armour dented, blackened an' 'oled. They were leaderless. They could no longer bring their guns to bear on us. Then the *Santa Anna*, 'oled below the water-line, slowly began to 'eel over to starboard. 'Er soldiers never 'ad a chance to fight. 'Undreds leapt into the sea to sink under the weight of their breastplates an' equipment!'

'I watched 'orrified an' then satisfied that the monster which 'ad 'oused me for them long 'ungry weeks 'ad met 'er end. 'An yet 'twere ne'er a pretty thing to watch a vessel die or to see men go along of 'er. Cap'n Martin leaned forward over the quarter rail.

"Well done lads! She's struck!"

Truly the long bold banners of King Philip of Spain were trailin' limply in the troubled water. Cries an' screams floated across the sea as the *Wrath* swam quietly by, 'er 'ands starin' solemn-like at the great battered 'ulk.

"To yer posts! Larboard guns stand by!"

Old John signalled the starboard crews to rest an' raised 'is 'and for the attention of the fresh crews.

"Fire!" 'e yelled.

The shots went whinin' across the deck of the *San Pedro.* John wanted 'er 'ull in one piece, the masts an' riggin' were the targets 'ere.'

'The resistance were poor. No 'eavy barrage answered us this time. Two an' four pounders opened up ragged but their aim were poor.

"Stand by to board!"

Snatchin' up cutlasses an' pistols our boardin' parties awaited the bump as the vessels come together.

Cap'n Martin shouted, "Keep the starboard guns closed up John an' keep an eye on the *Anna*!"

"Aye aye Sir," marked John.

Two boatloads of soldiers 'ad succeeded in leavin' the *Anna*, now 'eelin' over at an alarmin' angle, smoke pourin' from 'er stern.'

'With a slight bump, Mark brought the *Wrath* alongside the bullion vessel an' grapplin' irons were slung across an' made fast. With terrible cries, the boardin' party swarmed aboard the Spaniard meetin' the soldier's line with a fury of swingin' steel. The soldiers fell back leavin' their comrades tumblin' an' sprawlin'. Silent, 'is eyes almost closed, crouched an' moved forward, blades flickin' back and forth, claimin' a evil toll o' soldiery. Thomas, one 'and in 'is belt, was beatin' two soldiers back towards the quarterdeck with an ease that frightened the droppin's out o' 'is attackers. Diabalo pushed a giant of a fellow away from 'im, tuggin 'is fine curved blade out of 'is stomach. I saw a pirate fall awkwardly as a pike, thrown from aloft, impaled 'im to the deck. 'E tried to rise an' died 'mediately. The bulk of our boardin' party 'ad now cleared the main deck an' 'ad driven the soldiers to the starboard rail. One by one they were shoved into the oggin. Then the officers, led by Don Felipe, surrendered, bowin' from the 'igh poop an' unbucklin' their swords.

It were over.

Cap'n Martin, Amos an' I went across. Cap'n Martin received the Commander's sword an' escorted 'im aboard the *Wrath*. The boardin' party vanished below.'

'By the first bell of the middle, tons of gold, silver an' precious stones were stowed below on board the *Wrath*. The *Pedro* lay listless, 'er main topmast lyin' over the side in a tangle of riggin'. The *Anna* 'ad gone to the bottom, 'elped by another smokin' gift from twelve of John Craftesman's childer. Three boats 'ad got away into the empty wastes of the Caribbean as I'd done an' perhaps with more chance. Amos an' the Cap'n went below to get a final tally of the cargo an' to work out the shares. At first light the next mornin', after a little wine 'ad been taken, a much shaken Juan Felipe Fernandez was conducted back aboard 'is vessel an' cut adrift. Twenty 'ands went with 'im, all that were left of the crew of the *Pedro*. They were lucky fellows. Luckier than any English who might be unfortunate to fall into the 'ands of the Inquisition or to die aboard the galleys or on the plantations of Hispaniola.'

'After that voyage, I come ashore with two bar of gold, three of silver an' a bag of gold pistoles which I put away until I could see my way for'ard.'

Dick stretched. 'Bloody hell Andrew,' he said earnestly. 'I've been through many actions and many landings, often in the first wave but I've not heard a story like that before. I don't fancy the hand to hand business!'
Andrew nodded quietly. 'It weren't no 'igh day.'
Outside, the weather continued rough with the occasional squall riding wildly from the sea and battering the little town. It was one of those winds that tugged the leaves off trees and brought guttering and loose pantiles down into the streets and ghauts of Bay.

Dick knew the night was well on but he didn't feel tired. It was a rare occasion when he'd been the silent one and allowed someone else to dominate the conversation. It was usually he who was accused of dredging up the past and going on about the war years.

John Gilman '98

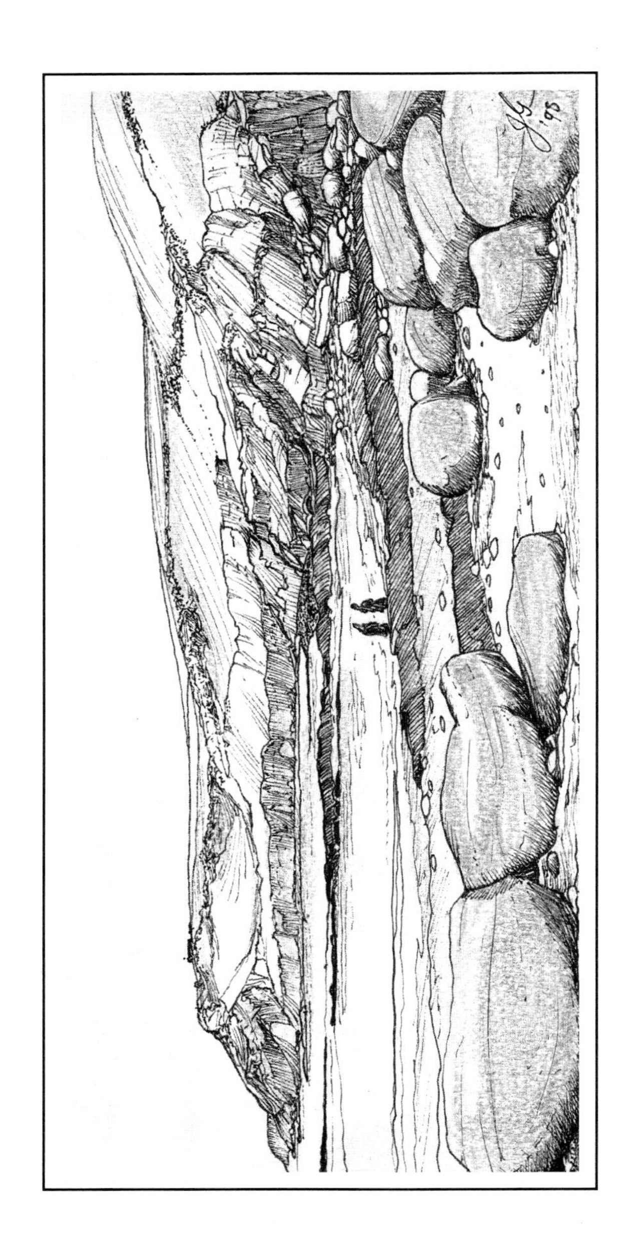

CHAPTER EIGHT

'We had some pretty scary times too and some near misses. I remember on one occasion we were at anchor in Salerno on the second trip of the first day. We'd loaded a Bofors detachment of the RAF Regiment and they had these weapons on the upper deck. They came in very useful as we unloaded and the enemy sheered off to other targets. When we'd finished, the skipper, Lieutenant Commander Page, had a strange hunch that we should move and he ordered the anchor to be raised and rang below for both engines to go full ahead. The anchor was hardly "up and down," when a stick of bombs blew a mighty hole in the shallows where we were just seconds ago. Had we not moved when we did, none of us would have survived to tell the tale.

'Andrew nodded. 'It's easy for the likes of us to share our times, 'cos we've both been in action in times of war. Not so easy for those who only 'ear us talkin' about it! Did you ever see anythin' very brave? Anyone who should 'ave got a medal or, in my day, a bar of silver?'

'A couple of times,' said Dick. 'The first was when we were on our way back from that Salerno trip. The RAF lads had left a huge pile of 40 millimetre Bofors ammunition up for'ard and just as we were about to dock we noticed that it was on fire, smoke was pouring out. Without thinking about his own safety, the Bosun, a Petty Officer from Bristol, ran up and started to claw his way to the base of the pile. He discovered the cause and flung it over the side and then commenced to ditch the rest. Undoubtedly he saved lives and a lot of potential damage. He didn't get anything more than a thankyou.'

'I were aware of your war,' returned Andrew. 'There were lots of convoys up an' down off 'ere particular at the beginnin'.'

Dick stood up, stretched and then settled down into the chair again and pushed his feet into the hearth.

'What happened after you got home, Andrew?'

'Well, after the good luck, come the bad. We 'ad one more trip in 'er an' then we lost 'er an' most of the lads too.'

Andrew rubbed both his hands roughly across his face and putting his head on one side, he looked Dick in the eye and said, 'I ought to tell 'ee, if you'm to understan' what I'm about. You see, I'm tryin' to lead up to a question I'm goin' to ask 'ee.'

'Go ahead, there's plenty of time.'

Andrew pursed his lips and squinted his eyes.

'I'm not so sure about that but I'll carry on while I 'ave the chance.'

'In common with all privateer skippers, Cap'n Martin knew that Spanish merchants bound across the Atlantic often joined up with armed escorts off the Azores. They'd been doin' this since the Isles, as they were called, come under the Spanish Crown back in 1581. This broke the long journey 'ome an' enabled them to ship fresh provisions, fresh water an' fruit. From the Azores they continued to Spanish waters, some goin' to Cadiz an' some goin' across the Bay to Bilbao. Long before 1581, the

Isles 'ad been a favourite cruising ground for Elizabeth's privateers an' so, after 'er triumOphant return from the Indies in the July of 1586 the *Wrath* joined several other fighting vessels on a voyage to the windward of Flores to see what they could catch.'

'So you shipped out on board the *Wrath of God* again?'

'Aye, I took Thomas' place as Mate. There were several new crew members on board that trip. Thomas, 'e stepped ashore on Redcliffe Wharf vowin' never to return to sea. "I shall carry the long boat anchor on me back," 'e beamed, "an' walk inland. When someone stops me an' asks whatever it is, there I will stay!" Of course 'e never did such a thing. Just said what generations of sailors 'ave been sayin' at the end of a voyage for a century of years! Amos was still Master of 'er an' there were a trust between us that 'ad become strong.'

Andrew stared deep into the embers of the fire whilst his voice continued deep, resonant and confident. He looked remarkably solid for a ghost and Dick had long suspended his disbelief. Here was a reliable ship-mate, a man of experience and knowledge and a person Dick felt he could trust too.

'Four days after leavin' the mouth of the Avon, preparations began towards puttin' the vessel into fightin' trim. Jason began to train one of the new 'ands on the staff. 'E were Tommy Baker from Bartholomew Street, Exeter, just inside the city wall. 'E were a lively little chap, full of fun an' game to try anythin'. The other new 'and were an experienced seaman from Porlock 'E 'ad been Master of a vessel for many years until 'is world crashed about 'im when 'is polacca were boarded an' 'is son taken by the

Spanish off Lundy. Now James Rawle wanted to sail against the Spanish an' 'ad left 'is cob cottage at Porlock Weir to do just that. Cap'n were doubtful about takin' 'im on until James asked, quiet like, for a brace of pistols. Cap'n calls for Gentleman. Gentleman, 'e comes up.

"You enquired for me?" he says.

"Yes. I wonder if you would oblige James 'ere by fetchin' your pistols?"

"Certain," replies Gentleman.

'E were back in a flash with 'is fancy wheel-lock pistols.

"Here," he proffered them to the Cap'n.

"Loaded an' ready?" says Cap'n.

"Certain," says Gentleman.

"See that knot-hole."

Gentleman lifted the pistol, sighted an' fired in one easy action.

The knot-hole vanished.

"An' now for long range," says Cap'n Martin, tossin' a kerchief over the side.

Gentleman 'eld the second pistol steady in both 'ands an' swung 'is arms, rigid agin the motion of the ship. There were a puff of smoke, a bang an' the kerchief were plucked below the waves. He then reloaded an' adjusted the pieces an' 'anded them to James. James felt the weight of both guns in 'is 'ands, dropped both arms an' then swung them up together. As they come up, 'e fired both at once an' two knot-'oles vanished in a shower of splinters a good ten yards beyond Gentleman's mark.

Cap'n, he looks at Gentleman. Gentleman smiles an' bows to James.

"Welcome aboard," says Cap'n.

"That were excellent shootin'," remarks Gentleman, "special as you were unfamiliar with the weight an' balance."

"I used to practice daily when I could afford to," grinned back James.

"We'll 'ave to find 'e a brace for yourself," declares Gentleman. There were a brace of longer barrelled Spanish 'andguns, silver inlaid, among the loot from the *Pedro*."

"That would be good," says James.

Says Cap'n. "You'd better direct your target practice over the side or Chips'll be after 'ee!" '

'The other vessels with us were Bar-boats as craft out the Taw an' Torridge estuary are called. They were excellent sea boats with superb sailin' qualities an' were not built as well anywhere in the South West. They carried above eighty guns atween 'em which made us a powerful fleet to be reckoned with in any action. Our fire power were not as great as a Spaniard, nor did we carry so large a crew. Few English vessels carried as many soldiers as the Spanish giants an' most privateers kept well clear of any engagement where this strength would be of account. Skilful swift sailing an' accurate gunnery were the most potent of our talents.'

'We worked up well and on the tenth day, ran into light airs. By six bells of the mornin' the followin' day, we was becalmed and the Cap'n orders us to stand easy. As you know, this is a time for us to relax an' take up our interests. Some played instruments, some played uckers, an' others carved wonderful models of ships. Some of us just yarned an' took a pipe of that new fangled baccy which 'ad come across from the colony. The comradeship an' fellow feelin' that prevailed on such occasions were one born out of adversity in the face of a common foe. Each man was an ally agin the Don, a friend to fight at one's side. A selflessness ruled on board, each man sharin' 'is possessions an' never wantin' for a helpin' 'and. Our tongues were often rough an' a good deal of leg pullin' went on but no man sought to see the distress of 'is neighbour.'

'Things haven't changed in that respect,' interrupted Dick. 'It's the big difference between the seaman and the landsman. No sailor would see his oppo short or duck out of an opportunity to help out whenever needed.'

'That's why I wanted to get through to you,' stressed Andrew. 'I need you to do something for me but you 'ave to understand the reason an' that is why you have to hear me out.'

'Go ahead. I'm listening,' answered Dick seriously.

'That night as lanthorns gleamed across the burnin' velvet of the summer Atlantic, music an' dancin' lilted into the stillness. Dancer toiled at 'is fiddle, bowin' away for all he was worth. Singin' followed as a runlet o' wine were passed around an' the crew joined in 'ymns an' songs. Strange 'ow us fellows, to all outward appearances, are supposed to be rough characters an' yet many are deep thinkin' an' serious minded. Perhaps we 'ad more time to think. Certain, the Reformation 'ad a great impact on common folk as it brought each man face to face with 'is Maker an' did away with Mother Church as a go-between. On t'other 'and it also threw a lot of comfort overboard an' left a lot of us mazed as to which were the right course to plot. Most of us were earnest believers an' opponents of the 'arsh methods of the Inquisition. Some 'ad been there an' been condemned to death in the galleys. Many of us 'ad been prisoners an' treated terrible bad; cut, beaten an' starved or worked to death.'

'At two bells of the first we turned to and sought to get the ship underway but it were eerie still an' there weren't a breath of air. Jason were on watch at the staff but it 'ad been lashed an' 'e was pacin' the quarterdeck with the Master. The vessel lay too quietly in the oily calm. As the night deepened the 'umidity increased an' the 'ands become restless. Through dawn the welkin stood dark. It were unusual warm an' lookin' thick an' black. Little puffs of wind ruffled the water here an' there. Amos recognised the signs. We all did. By three bells of the forenoon, the *Wrath* 'ad been shortened down to reefed fore an' main tops'ls. Double lashin's were put on the boats an' the 'atch covers double secured. The other vessels were seen to follow suit.'

'Suddenly the expected squall 'it 'er an' she 'eeled over to starboard 'mong a welter of green an' white water. 'Er bows sank deep into the 'issin' sea as she began to run away afore the wind.

"Way ho!" shouted Jason, smilin' fit to bust. "This be better!"

After the sticky indolent hours of still airs the *Wrath* were soon buckin' an' plungin' through the swollen wind-tore ocean. All of us was feelin' the 'zileration of movement after calm. 'Owever, Amos knew that the weather could worsen. We soon lost sight of the other craft. By the afternoon watch we could make out the lines of a Spaniard, shortened down like ourselves an' runnin' free a mile or so on the larboard bow.

"Don on the larboard bow there!" yelled Amos. "Runnin' away afore the wind."

Cap'n Martin, who 'ad come on deck, took 'is skri-glass to 'er.

"Don right enough. She'll not trouble us though."

"More's the pity," slipped in Jason, still smilin'.

'The wind increased. The *Wrath* continued to slip swiftly through the 'eavy seas, a tribute to 'er builders an' a delight to 'andle. A giant stern sea ran at our 'eels bearin' the leanin' vessel afore it, always yards away. Wind screamed an' whistled among the stays an' spindrift like a 'uge slow movin' curtain swung across the deck from the rollin' peaks.'

'The seas were splendid. 'Undreds of 'eavin' tons of movin' water bearin' us up to a thick lowerin' sky an' drawin' us back to view only walls of livin' ocean as the vessel run 'igh across each crest an' deep into each shudderin' trough. Riggin' stood taut as bar iron, canvas like stone.

"It's still risin'!" screamed Jason over the frenzy.

Amos nodded, 'is eyes aloft.

'Twere still very warm. Water streamed down Jason's face from 'is spray-soaked 'air. 'Is shirt were plastered to 'is back.'

'Then the first great flash, crack o' levin, thunder split the dark sky into a thousand shards an' the rain sheeted down. The watch on deck 'uddled under the bulwarks. Amos gulped great mouthfuls of fresh water as the colder rain splashed fully in 'is face off the furled spanker. Crash after crash of ear-piercin' thunder bounced off the risin' sea. Vivid splashes of levin slayed about the 'eavens as the *Wrath* ploughed 'er way afore the wind with 'undreds o' miles of open sea before 'er. Cap'n Martin made 'is way to the staff.

"What's the ship's 'ead?"

"We're runnin' due sou'west," shouted back Jason. "Wind's a true nor'easter!"

"Amos!" directs Cap'n. "I don't want to lose too much leeway. Can ye come up into the wind a little?"

"Not yet Cap'n, unless we get the tops'ls off 'er an' 'eave to."

The Cap'n nodded.

"Let me know the moment the wind slackens."

"Aye aye Sir," returned the old man.

'E turned to Jason, "Let 'er drive, son."

The *Wrath* drove on into the first night o' the gale.'

'Mid day the morrow saw us feelin' a might sorry for us-selves. Old Amos 'ad proved right in 'is judgement an' the storm 'ad developed into a full roarin' gale. You know what I mean, it's 'ard to describe to a landsman. To say a 'uge movin' sea become mountains an' valleys would not be strong enough. Acres o' troubled water took up the most grotesque an' terrifyin' shapes as they surged an' threatened the vessel. 'Twere 'ard to speak. The noise prevented any spoken communication on deck. Even if the shriek of the gale didn't drown every attempt to speak, then the wind whipped the sound away from our empty mouths.'

'Jason 'ad gone below hours since, 'is wound troublin' 'im by the excessive movement. I took the staff an' it took all my years of experience to 'andle the stubborn bugger across the bloody great crests. She were beginnin' to tire. One o' the boats 'ad vanished, takin' a fifteen foot section of bulwark with it. The decks were constantly awash with green boilin' water pourin' about the plankin'. Cap'n Martin come on deck.

"Reckon we've lost near a 'undred miles!" he screamed into my face through cupped 'ands.

"All o' that!" I yelled back, but my voice were carried away.

"We'll 'eave to!"

Amos looked doubtful. The crests were too steep an' she stood every chance o' rollin' over as she come about. Cap'n Martin went over to Amos an' the pair of 'em went below.

'Twere decided to get all sail off 'er afore they blew out, stream two sea anchors an' come about 'ead to wind. Crew lurched across the deck grippin' the lifelines. Slowly the tops'ls were let out an' clewed up, men strainin' on the swollen 'aul-yards as they laboured through the blocks. Sea after sea crashed across their backs as they bent to their task. The sea anchors were made ready an' a group o' men were busy makin' fast the inboard end of the cables. Then Amos signalled to stream 'em an' the quartermaster to put the 'elm 'ard over. Staff were no good 'ere an' we used tackles on the 'elm. This were the critical moment.'

'She topped a foamin' 'ogback an' slid, turnin' into a trough. The sea anchors dropped away. Tops'l yards secured. The 'elm 'ard over. Slowly she come round, 'eelin' over at an alarmin' angle. Flyin' sea-spit thrashed across 'er decks. The crew were 'urled, tumblin' bruised an' gaspin' into the scuppers. Then the bows rose 'igher an' 'igher as the next giant began to make for the vessel. God's teeth! Up an' up till 'er wild movement were checked by the sea anchors an' she rode bows on to the frightenin' seas.'

'Another day passed, makin' over twenty four hours since any o' the crew 'ad enjoyed a meal. About the only place on board that were still dry were the powder store, double-planked, sealed an' well below the water line. Gradual, as the day wore on, the seas went down an' the sky broke up, uncoverin' ragged patches of deep blue. Visibility increased to reveal a small foreign vessel 'ove to about a league away on the weather bow. Of our own fleet there were no sign. Almost as sudden as it 'ad begun, the wild weather swept away, its torn dark edge contrastin' with the brilliant blue of the late afternoon sky.

"Bit fresh that," says Amos.

"Set us back a mile or so an' perhaps a day or two to clear up this gallimaufry," indicated the Cap'n, jerkin' 'is thumb at the damage.

"Two days," declared Chips, appearin' from below. "Two days at the most." '

'The deck steamed. Clothes-lines appeared 'zif by magic. Cap'n Martin, Amos an' Chips conned the wreckage.

"Better renew those boat lashin's before we lose any more," pointed out Amos, noddin' toward the ship's boats saggin' among a tangle of broken chocks an' twisted cordage.

"Vessel on the larboard quarter!" come a cry.
Cap'n Martin looked up.
"Can't be the vessel we saw just now."
"Movin' up fast Cap'n."
Cap'n regained the quarterdeck an' took 'is skri-glass to the stranger.
"There's two of 'em. Could mean trouble."
'E 'anded the glass to Amos who 'ad moved up beside 'im. Amos peered at the vessels through the glass. Two Spaniards were makin' up fast towards the *Wrath.* They were both under a 'eavy press o' sail. Crew were movin about on deck an' Amos swore 'e could see a glint o' steel now an' again as a soldier turned into the lowerin' sun.

'Andin' the glass back to the Cap'n, Amos took a sight on the strengthenin' sun as it rode through the few remainin' rags o' cloud.
'E looked up.
"We're right in the middle of the Bay of Biscay. About 'undred an' eighty mile due south of Ushant as near as damn it!"
'Then those yonder are regular patrol vessels,' I ventured.
"An' lookin' for such as ourselves," says Cap'n. "Caught after 'eavy weather on a lee shore. We'll try an' outrun 'em. Amos get sail on 'er an' we'll try to make away to the windward of 'em."
Amos nodded an' detailed the Quartermaster.
"Steer west-nor-west."
"Aye, Master, west-nor-west it is." '
'With a crack, the canvas of the main courses broke out into the wind. The *Wrath* went about, 'er decks crowded

as both watches turned to, preparin' the ship to fly. The gap between the vessels lessened. The Dons altered course to try an' cut us off from makin' it to the open sea. Battle seemed inevitable as the vessels closed. We certainly wanted to avoid action in our present damaged state. Our crew was weary and dog-tired after the constant buffetin' o' the gale. It looked 'zif the only course open to us were to fight or run away before the wind.

"If we've got to fight," says Amos, "we mustn't allow the Spanish to get both larboard an' starboard of us. We'll alter course to run across their bows."

"Steer nor-nor-west."

Tops'ls an' t'gans'ls billowed out into the breeze, still fresh from the nor-east. The sea smacked against 'er windward side as she punched 'er way through the waves.

"Keep 'er closer," urges Amos.

"It's gonner be close," says Cap'n.

" 'Nother course open to us is to run away to le'ward an' bank on losin' 'em after nightfall."

"We'll try this first. We might just make it!" says Cap'n grimly. The gap lessened, the *Wrath* only cables ahead.

"Steer true Quartermaster."

"True north it is Cap'n."

God's blood Dick, we was closer to the wind than I'd thought possible. But we 'eld an' made it! Foiled of makin' a broadside attack, the Dons opened fire from their bow-chasers an' top-pieces. Luckily, sea were by no means quiet an' the shots was sinkin' wide an' short, kickin' up 'igh splashes. The next ragged salvo went 'igh an' for'ard. Their swivel-guns 'awked an' barked, puffs o' smoke clearin' away toward us. A few balls tore over'ead.'

'We was through. Another mile or two on the same course would be enough to lose the buggers an' make a break for open sea. Darkness were beginnin' to fall an' the wind to freshen once more. We was now out o' range an' very pleased to be so. Ol' John Craftesman 'adn't even unlashed one o' the *Wrath*'s guns since the storm an' they remained lashed securely to their ring-bolts, the ports tightly closed an' daubed with pitch. During the evenin' the wind come around in our favour, enablin' us to put a good league between us an' our enemy.'

'Cap'n sent a reluctant 'and to the mainmast truck to keep a careful look-out for any more vessels in the area. The evenin' passed slowly, bell followin' bell until fully eight bells o' the first. Amos kept 'is place by the rail watchin' the vessel's 'ead. The watch changed an' the lookout lowered 'imself stiffly 'and over 'and down the ratlines.

" 'Sdeath," he mouthed, "it's woundy cold aloft!"

"Nothin' at all?" enquired Amos.

"Empty as a boneyard after dark!"

The fresh watch come on deck an' another 'and was detailed aloft.

"Best take your sea-coat with 'ee," said Amos quietly.

The wind blew fitfull all night, sometimes fearful strong an' sometimes 'ardly at all. Amos kept 'is post an' the 'ands busy trimmin' the vessel to every change. I kept the staff. Between us we used every trick o' seamanship to push 'er out further into the Atlantic and safety. As dawn spread about the eastern 'orizon, the lookout were able to 'ave a good see round.

"What do you see?" shouted Amos.

"All clear!"

"Very good, stay aloft till sun-up an' I'll send up an 'and to replace you."

'E waited until the lookout acknowledged an' then turned to me.

"When us gets a definite sun we'll make out our position again but by my reckonin' we're safe now."

'E grinned.

"First time I've ever run away from a Spaniard!"

"I shan't tell anyone!" says I.'

'All that day the crew worked steady to bring the *Wrath* back into fightin' trim. The first job was to cut away all the torn an' tangled cordage. Then the ship were cleaned down from stem to stern to wash away the salt encrusted on every surface. Next the guns an' carriages was overhauled, cleaned an' greased. Some of the tackles was split apart. These needed skilled 'ands to replace.Then Chips 'ad the task of replacin' fifteen foot of bulwark made up of seasoned ellum planks on oak frames. The lines o' washin' come out again as the crew off watch got their own gear in order. In the galley, Cook were preparin' the first 'ot meal for three days. There were no kickshaws on board the Wrath but Cap'n asked Cook to do 'is best. At seven bell o' the afternoon there come a shout from the top.

"Vessel fine on the starboard bow!"

The bustle on deck stopped as the 'ands stopped work to gave out to sea. Amos 'ailed the man aloft.

"Is 'er a Spaniard?"

"No, 'er's British built!"

Cap'n Martin studied the rig and passed 'is glass to Amos.

"Here, what do ee make of er?"

"It's one of our fleet, its *Seaventure*!"

"That's what I thought."

Seaventure it was. Slowly we come up on 'er. 'Er bulwarks was missin down 'er entire starboard side. She were flyin' 'er pennant upside-down signifyin' a loss of life on board. When she come within a cable's length it were possible to see the crew standin' listless about 'er decks like gallicrows.

"Something gravely wrong there," indicated Amos.

As the two ships come together we could see that none of the gale damage 'ad been put to rights. She were under sail but that were all. The decks were a shambles, both boats gone, 'atch covers splintered, decks split an' the staff torn out its mountin's.'

'We seldom came into Liverpool with boats intact,' said Dick. 'North Atlantic convoys in winter used to play hell with the light skiffs carried on a corvette.'

Andrew nodded and continued. 'With a bump, the *Wrath* come alongside an' Cap'n an' Amos went aboard of 'er.

"Where's the Cap'n an' the Master?"

"Over the side," replied a sailor without moving from 'is seat on a broken 'atch cover.

"Up man!" says Cap'n sharp like.

"Sir," replied the man, standin' up.

"What 'appened to your officers?"

"Overboard, Sir. We was struck by a giant sea. You might say we was almost pooped. Broke over the stern it did an' snatched the rails, bulwarks, several crew, the Cap'n an' the Master over the side in a trice."
"We'll see the Mate then."
"Gone," returned the sailor, "Missin' in the night."
Cap'n shook 'is 'ead.
"Send for the Bosun."
The Bosun limped up, 'is leg lashed between two belayin' pins. 'E apologised, greetin' the Cap'n.
"Sorry about this," he started. "We've not the 'eart to start the repairs. I'm not fit to stand long."
He smiled painfully. "There's others 'urt too."
Cap'n took 'im by the arm an' sat 'im down. He thought a minute.
"Ow many were lost over the side?"
"Five 'ands, Sir," he replied, "that is beside the Cap'n, Master an' Mate."
"You'd better show me their marks in the ship's papers later."
"Then there was the lad."
"The lad?"
"Aye," went on the Bosun, "the little lad. 'Is first voyage. 'E were thirteen."
Amos looked grim.
"Who got way on 'er after the storm?"
"I did, Master, set a course which I 'oped would steer us clear o' the Spanish." 'E looked from one to the other.
"Trouble is, I'm not much of an 'and at navigation an' I wasn't sure where us were. I was very pleased to see it were you Sir." '

'Cap'n Martin made a decision.

"We'll take 'er 'ome Amos. Get Andrew on board as Master. We'll keep company with 'er to Plymouth."

'E turned to the Bosun.

"We'll put a man in command an' we'll escort you back home."

Cap'n Martin started to stride down the length of the crippled vessel.

"Best let Chess look to the injured. You've certainly taken a thrashin'." 'E went to the edge of the deck to look at the splintered roots of the bulwarks. 'E shook 'is 'ead an' signalled for me to come over.

"Andrew, I'm givin' you this command. See what you can do to tidy 'er up a bit. Sort through the papers an' find out what you can about 'er owners. Call a roll an' check the crew lists. Find out if there is a chippy on board. We'll act as escort an' keep a look out for any sign of the *Black Swan* or the *Lynmouth.*"

The Bosun appeared again, 'oppin' on one leg.

"Beg your pardon, Sir."

The Cap'n turned.

"Did you mention the *Lynmouth* Sir?"

"I did."

"No good keepin' a look-out for 'er Sir. 'Er's gone down. We was close by at the time. We 'ave five of 'er 'ands on board, includin' the Master's Mate."

"Then why the..."

" 'E's down below Sir, 'ad a crack over the 'ead. 'E's not well enough to work the vessel. Sails sewed 'im up Sir."

The more I thought about it, the more I were grateful for a sound vessel an' a good crew. Compared with the *Seaventure,* the *Wrath* 'ad come through unscathed.

"What of the *Black Swan?"*

"Nary a thing, Sir. We lost sight of 'er in the first hour, same's yourself Sir."

Cap'n thanked 'im. Turnin' to me, 'e says,

"Set a course for Plymouth Andrew. We'll be close but in case we become parted through bad weather, that's our destination. We can re-fit there and renew our stores."

The Cap'n an' Amos left the vessel. Silent returned with my gear. The injured men were transferred to the *Wrath,* then the ships swung away from each other an' I were left wi' a cripple to nurse.'

'We set a course for Plymouth an' arrived without any trouble six days later. That voyage ended a run of 'apchance an' 'eralded a patch of ill luck which were to last for a number o' years. We never saw the *Black Swan* again but we 'eard that young Wyndham 'ad managed to bring 'er into Appledore where I believe she were rebuilt.'

It seemed very quiet outside and the wind had dropped. Andrew had been looking uneasy for a while, casting glances over his shoulder and tilting his head to one side.

'I haven't long Dick. I trust I'll be able to meet with 'ee again shortly.'

Dick rose and went across to the window. He pulled the curtain aside and peered out. King Street was dark and the wind had decreased. He was no longer aware of the insistent buffeting or the dull roar of the sea. He turned just in time to see the indistinct outline of Andrew fade away. He smiled to himself and yawned. Then he resumed his seat and stretched. In less than two minutes he was asleep. It was six thirty and Sylvia would be up in half an hour.

John Gilman '98.

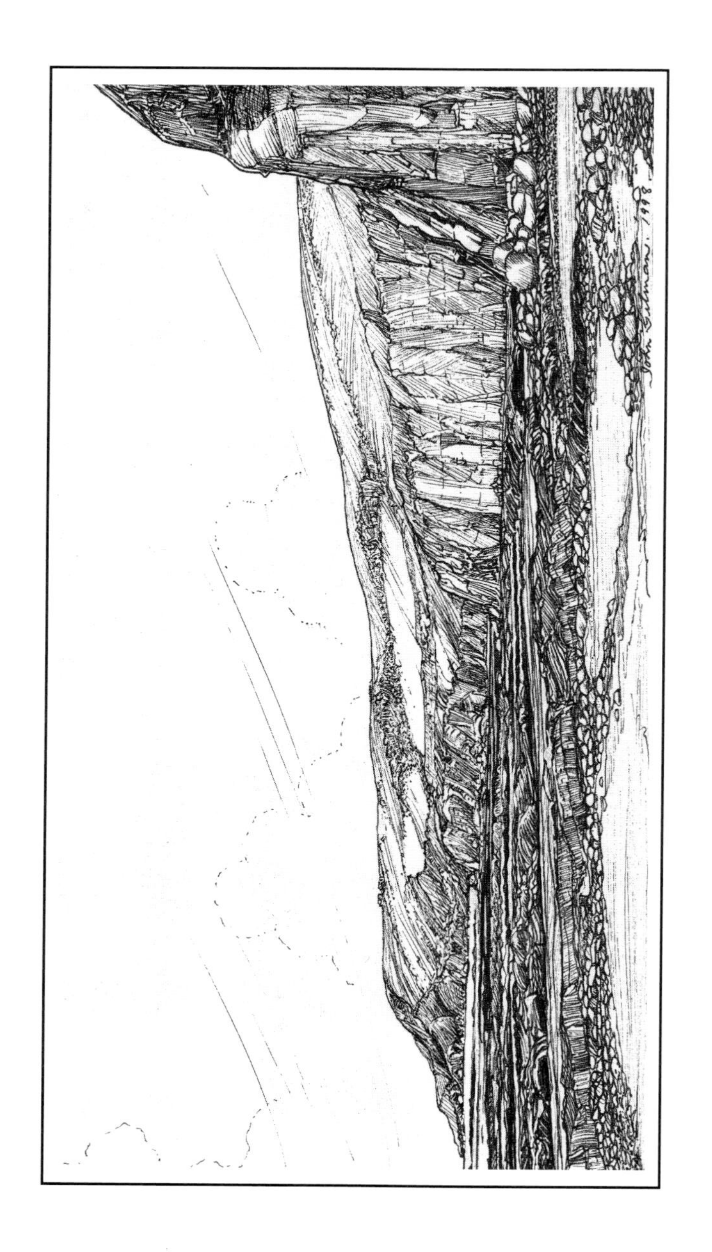

CHAPTER NINE

Michael looked long and hard up the beach. There was no movement except the growing mist of sea spume that obscured the far rocky outline of Peak. All the visitors had left the beach, the last having just climbed up the slipway below him. It was Dick Jordan-Squires. He'd had his daughter with him and Dick had introduced her. He thought that Dick had invited him to join them in the Bay Hotel for a drink but he must have made his excuses for here he was straining his eyes for one last indication of an elusive reality that had been a part of his life for decades. He'd turned and caught Annie's eye just as she entered the hotel and registered her inquisitive empathy. Just how he was aware of her sensitivity he couldn't fathom. It was one of those intuitive judgements that often proved to be right. He thought he'd seen her about Bay during past summers when he'd been here but he'd not spoken. His visits were always taken up with other matters.

It was a strange story and one that spanned the years since his first visits in the early sixties. One day he'd have to tell someone about it all but right now he was still too confused to accept what his conscious mind told him was now a part of his reality.

The real and the unreal, history and propaganda, myth and legend were all very much a part of Michael's daily bread as he attempted in his teaching and writing to draw concrete distinctions between them. He'd been well aware from a very early age that a popular reality was a very personal construct beginning in the home and extending into the community. The challenge of what is and what was had always stimulated him, which of course was why he'd opted for history as a subject. Once in academic circles he'd had the opportunity to trade ideas and hypotheses with colleagues and he found that exciting. When it was his turn to engage in research, he'd chosen the period towards the end of World War Two when there had supposedly existed a period of co-operation and unity in the United Kingdom. Michael's task had been to examine whether this was fact, myth or propaganda or a blend of all three. He'd tackled the question as a realist with a scientific approach and had, or so he'd thought, come to some sound conclusions.

His own personal life however was not as well ordered for over the years he had to admit allowing certain inconsistencies into his perceptions. The girl at Robin Hood's Bay was the problem.

The holiday of 1967 was the turning point. He was thirty one that summer and just starting a new job at Oxford. He'd come up to Bay early in June and taken a cottage in Brig Garth for two months. He'd brought reading material with him and of course, he'd do some writing too. He couldn't say that he'd forgotten that fleeting glimpse of an elusive girl under Stoup Beck some years past but she certainly wasn't the motivation that took him out on to the beach and scaurs for more time than he'd intended. Of course he loved it here. As the summers of the fifties blended into the summers of the sixties the passing of the years meant nothing in the town and on the beach. It was always the same and encouraged the fantasy of a place out of time where society's relentless wheel had no crushing power. Boy and man, buckets and spades or books and thoughts, here was the perfect place to escape time.

It was a Friday. He remembered that. He'd been struck with the idea that he'd like to try some fishing. Of course it was after reading Leo Walmsley's *So Many Loves* in which Leo extolled the delights of fishing with his friend Captain Bunny. And so, discovering that he could hire a pulling boat from a local resident, he'd got help down the slip and launched it about an hour before high water. The weather was fine and the sea quite calm. Slowly he pulled out alongside the scaurs until he reached deep water and the freedom to choose where to go for his fishing. It ought to be said that at the time Michael was no sailor or did he have any knowledge of the foreshore beyond reading about it. There was an anchor in the boat and several fathoms of line and he thought that he would proceed down the coast towards Ravenscar, anchor and then fish from the boat for an hour or two before returning to the beach below the slip or, if the tide had gone down a bit, to the sandy spit between the scaurs that ran out beyond the Bay Hotel where the local boats came in. It didn't seem a bad plan.

Accordingly, Michael pulled awkwardly down the shore past Stoup Beck Sands and Low Balk keeping a sharp eye out for rocks for he didn't want to put a hole in the boat if he could avoid it. The first half hour went splendidly and the light clinker-built boat seemed to move easily through the water. After slack water, she seemed to move even more easily and Michael congratulated himself that he was making excellent progress. As the ebb strengthened, a short, sharp sea began to slap the boat causing it to jerk and make his progress a little more erratic. He seemed to be a bit further out that he'd wished. Glances over his shoulder confirmed that he needed to be closer inshore and so he bent himself to the task of bringing the boat back closer to the beach under Miller's Nab but he was still wary of the rising spray that told him there were rocks curving off the shore in parallel bands at this point.

Although the sun still blazed and on the far beach he could see groups of holiday-makers sunbathing and paddling, out here it was decidedly choppy as a breeze developed with the ebb tide. Redoubling his efforts, he pulled for the shore but didn't seem to be making much progress. Perhaps it was time to anchor. He was beginning to feel tired.

Shipping his oars, he stood up and stooping, went forward to the bow where the anchor lay on a coil of rope. He lifted it and balanced it on the side of the boat before allowing it to slip over the side. Down it went with the rope snaking after it until the tail end of the rope vanished from sight. Alarmed, he turned just in time to see one of his oars slip gently through the rowlock into the sea leaving him adrift with one oar and no anchor. Panic was the one thing he knew he should not do and yet waves of fear seemed to hit him under the ribs and he sat down to think what to do.

Grabbing the remaining oar, he replaced the leather in the rowlock and started to pull but it didn't do more than send him turning and turning about as the shore seemed to move of its own volition further and further away. 'The sensible thing,' he thought, 'would be to get up into the bows and use the oar as a paddle on both sides.' This Michael did and to his relief, it seemed to check his movement towards the rocks at the base of Peak under Ravenscar now looming much closer than before. It was a temporary relief however as, tiring with the unaccustomed effort, he was forced to give up and rest. He was however a little closer inshore and might, with luck, manage to get to the beach between the outcrops.

It was then he became aware of someone else in the drama. He looked about him. Of course there was no-one in the boat and his quick glance around confirmed that there were no other craft in the vicinity. Sinking back on the forward thwart he looked over the side and sat up with a jolt.

It was the girl. There was no doubt about it. If there was time to think, perhaps he would have done so. Certainly she registered with a distinct shock. What should he make of it? She held on to the side of the boat with one hand and looked up at him with concern and understanding. Her long brown hair was plastered against her face as the water dashed into her eyes and ran streaming down her cheeks. 'I think I can help.' Her voice sounded confident. 'I've seen it done a score of times. Use the oar over the stern! Put it in that little groove and move it from side to side. It's called sculling the boat. It'll move you in a straight line. Or better than you've been doing!'

Michael took the oar to the stern and kneeling up in the stern sheets tried to do as he was told.

'No, not that way! Stand up and use both hands, like in a figure of eight. Make the blade of the oar push like a screw!'

In sheer desperation Michael grasped the idea and soon found that it worked.

'I'll keep an eye on your course. You concentrate on sculling. And don't stop until I tell you!'

Slowly the boat eased into calmer water. Gradually it moved on a diagonal course towards the shore, slipping beween the dark ridges that supported the wilder water that surged about the rocky crests. Michael began to get the hang of it and felt confident enough to look over his shoulder. The girl was on the landward side of the boat, her left arm out of the water holding on, guiding it between the scaurs. Sometimes the sea broke over her head and she almost vanished from sight.

'Fifty yards and we've made it!' she cried. 'Get some of the people to help you drag the boat up the beach.'

Michael redoubled his efforts and ran into the shallows on a tiny patch of clean sand alongside Billet Scaur, the bows chewing into the sea-soaked, puddling tide-line. He jumped out of the boat, grabbed the bow, and heaved it as hard as he could from the broken waves that ran up the streaming gulley. The tide was going out. The boat was safe for the moment. He looked up the beach and saw a group of boys advancing towards him. They would help.

The relief was past expression. He was safe. He'd been rescued by the girl!

Where was the girl? Before the boys got to him he looked carefully up and down the shoreline. He was further down the beach than he usually ranged. Of the girl there was no sign. As before, she'd mysteriously slipped away.

Two of the lads agreed to go ahead to Bay and arrange for a motor boat to tow his boat back. For half a crown another volunteered to stay with the boat until help arrived. As for Michael, he resolved to learn something about boats and how to handle them and to discover the nature of Bay beyond the tide-line in case he ever ventured out again. What was a priority however was to discover who the girl was and to thank her for saving his life. In 1967, Michael couldn't swim.

Later that evening when all had been sorted out and he'd listened carefully to the advice of the boat owner, he'd gone back to Brig Garth and re-lived his day. He wasn't very proud of himself and realised that there was a world of knowledge he needed to acquire before he set out on such an adventure again. He then set to thinking about the girl. Thank God she'd arrived when she did. It was only then that he realised something strange about her. Out there in the Bay, she hadn't been in a swimming costume. She was dressed in a longish skirt with buttons down the front and a simple long-sleeved blouse. In fact he could have sworn she'd been wearing something similar when he'd seen her before.

Despite spending long wind-burned hours on the beach and more than a few salt-spattered afternoons learning how to sail he discovered no trace of the girl. He would have liked to have thanked her properly. After some weeks he concluded that she must have gone home on the Saturday following his embarrassing adventure. Despite her unusual appearances and even more abrupt disappearances he still clung to the idea that she could be no other than a shy, solitary personality who, for reasons of her own, preferred not to become involved in casual or lengthy conversations. As for her clothing, well, there were plenty of holiday makers who paddled out further than a few feet and spent the rest of the day allowing their clothes to dry on their backs. If she'd seen him in distress and realised the situation perhaps she'd plunged straight in without forethought. This made sense.

Now that he'd had some proper tuition and made a close study of the chart of Robin Hood's Bay he realised what a fool he'd been. Prior knowledge of tides and currents plus a good understanding of what was on the sea-bed underneath would have made all the difference. Perhaps next year he'd try again but this time make sure all his gear was secure. He'd put up with a good deal of leg pulling in the Dolphin and heard the two main choruses over and over again.

'You were lucky not to have been swept out to sea!

'You were lucky you didn't pile up on the rocks!'

'Never mind, I deserved them,' he mused. He was lucky. Lucky that someone was at hand to guide him in between the scaurs in a choppy sea and to show him how to propel a boat with a single oar. Of course he'd told the story that a swimmer had guided him ashore but the locals seemed sceptical about the possibility of anyone swimming that far down the Bay unless of course, they were silly visitors who didn't know any better.

It was in his final week that he decided to walk down the beach for the last time that year. He'd climb up from Stoup Beck and find the path that led up the side of the hill to the road. It was a warm, balmy day with a gentle sea breeze. It had rained in the night and there were patches of wet sand here and there and extending from under the heaps of blackened bladderwrack, summer-dry above the shingle. There were few folk about and he had the beach to himself for most of his walk. He'd planned the lectures for the coming term and his research was going well so the day was his.

He loved this shore and just couldn't resist trying to put his thoughts into words. He was no poet but the sheer beauty and impact of this coastline often made him wish he was better with words. Sometimes they just flowed into his head and he wished afterwards that he had scribbled them down on a bit of paper to make better sense when he got home. On other occasions, try as hard as he could, there just weren't words to capture what he'd experienced and he'd felt tongue-tied and inarticulate.

Today, as he strode along the ever-changing, familiar, much-loved sandy trackways between the shingle and the scaurs, words again sought lodging in his mind and he thought that this time he might try to remember a couple of sentences at least. Whether they would remain with him long enough for him to write down when he got home was the question and whether they would be worth anything was another.

There is a cleanness after
Wind and sky-pressed water rears
Upon the shore and leaves
No creature marks save
What we and a
Single strutting heron bring
Into Bay.

There is a stillness after
Storm when sullen surges thrust
Between the scaurs and mark
The channel courses where
We and a
Bright blue painted coble might
Enter Bay.

He was nearing the brow of the footpath as it climbed across the first ridge still quite close to the beach and above a drop of eighty feet or so, when he spotted a lonely figure sitting on the cliff top in a circle of grass some thirty yards to his left. At first he thought it couldn't be, then he thought it might and so he slowed and stopped before deliberately leaving the path to close the gap between them. He never let his eyes leave her. This time he wouldn't lose her. Closer and closer he came. She knew he was coming but she stayed quite still, sitting hunched there, her knees up and her arms loosely clasped about them. She was looking away over towards Bay before turning her head towards him.

'I come here often. It's a favourite place of mine.'

She continued, smiling.

'I've never sculled a boat you understand, just seen it done. It seemed the logical thing to do under your circumstances.'

'I wanted to find you, to thank you.'

'Don't mention it. Glad I could help.'

Michael swallowed and dropped to his knees alongside her. He turned and looked full at her.

'You are a pretty elusive character,' he started, 'I've searched Bay from top to bottom and couldn't find you. Where are you staying?'

'Oh, here in Bay. I spend all my summers here.'

'I do too,' replied Michael warmly. 'I must confess I love it.'

'I thought you did. Bay is for special people. There's a lot more to Bay than meets the eye.'

Michael sat back on his heels and started to relax. She didn't seem in a hurry to escape this time and he felt that the ice had been broken. He longed to fire a barrage of questions at her to find out who she was and where she came from and why she had chosen to come back regularly to Bay but felt somehow tongue-tied. He who could talk for an hour non-stop in the lecture theatre and handle questions with confidence felt the words slipping away and a growing content to be sitting passively here on the cliff top beside her. He smiled at her and a little hesitantly she ruefully smiled back.

She spoke. 'I've seen you about for a number of years now. You were nearly always alone and seemed pretty confident and self contained. Tell me, are you happy here?'

'Why yes, I suppose I am. For me, Bay has a certain magic, a charm that transcends the present so that whenever I come here I enter a world that probably means more to me than the one outside. You know, the country over the hill where it all goes on. Yes, I'm happy here.'

She held him in her gaze. It was the first time that their eyes had met with meaning. 'I had to ask you that. Can I ask you another question?'

'Fire away,' urged Michael.

She approached her question with some reticence and lowered her voice.

'Tell me,' she urged, 'have you ever had any problems with relationships or in trusting others unwisely?'

It seemed an important issue to her and Michael paused to consider his reply.

'I was married once. That was a problem of relationships in which I was too immature to gauge the outcomes. It only lasted a short time and our interests separated us pretty quickly. I tend to trust people intuitively and fully. It's got me into trouble on one or two occasions. If I'm honest, I'm probably better as a loner. I've plenty of work to do that interests me and I prefer to come here when I require solitude or peace.'

She nodded slowly.

'My problems were pretty overwhelming. I trusted easily and was badly hurt. Like you, I find here the peace and tranquillity that blots out the pain of betrayal. You are the first person I've spoken to in a long while. You see, I'm not going back.'

Michael felt the weight of compassion surge within him and he hoped that he could somehow show her that he wanted to be there for her. It wasn't that she'd saved his life, it was a warm and tender feeling that he wished he could wrap around her in her sadness.

'Look,' said Michael, 'I mean this sincerely. If you need a friend or just someone to talk to please come to me. I have no wish to pry or intrude into your life but I would like to help if it is at all possible.'

He reached out to her, his hand stopping just short of her arm. He went on.

'We seem to share a genuine love of this place. Perhaps we can share our thoughts and our feelings too.'

'I don't know how it will work,' she replied, 'but I hope we can meet again. I need to talk and to try to put my life in perspective. One thing is certain, I'm not going back.'

Michael thought for a while. He would have to go back, and soon. There was a life out there for him and work that needed doing but he could accept that for some, the pain of that other life across the hill was too acute and they had to make decisions. Bay was so right for the folk who loved it and in many ways he envied those who'd made the decision to leave the rat-race and take up the quieter life away from the pressures, the urgency and the impositions of modern living.

After sitting for an hour, they rose together and resuming the path, wandered on up the hill stopping now and again to look at the view. There was no denying that Michael felt drawn to her. It seemed so right. From what he understood, she'd had a pretty difficult time. She told him that she'd been married and that her husband had deserted her after taking everything she had. Michael had felt a powerful indignation that anyone could treat so gentle a girl in this fashion. 'That was it,' he thought, 'she was a gentle creature, ingenuous and trusting. It shone from her, even now after the things that had happened to her.' He resolved that if it was possible, he'd try to be her strength and comfort.

As they climbed easily into the sunshine he tried again to impress upon her that he was in earnest.

'I meant what I said earlier,' he pressed. 'I would like to be your friend.'

She swung around to face him.

'I don't know what your name is.'

'It's Michael.'

'Well, Michael, this is a big step forward for me, bigger than you realise, and I'm not sure how it will work out. I accept your offer of friendship but again, I'm not making any promises.'

'And your name?' asked Michael gently.

'Sara,' she said.

They walked on in silence and it was sufficient.

For Michael, the day swung giddily overhead. He felt elated and at the same time anxious for the new responsibility he felt for his part in the infant friendship. He'd not said anything as important for a number of years and he didn't want this relationship to founder as easily as his last. On the other hand he didn't want to blunder into her life and be the cause of further hurt. He vowed to be careful and as sensitive as he could be.

Within the hour they reached the top road and the sudden impact of that world they had touched on. Cars in groups of three and four swept by and a slower bus laboured up the deceptive incline from the Scarborough direction. Sara stopped still for a while and then crossed the road and stood a little apprehensively on the verge as if looking out for something. She then lifted her head, brushed both hands through her hair, smiled with that same rueful look he'd seen before and rejoined him.

'Shall we go back through Fylingthorpe?'

They set off along the road.

John Gilman '93.

CHAPTER TEN

Those early years were full of wonder. After busy terms and for the whole summer vacation he returned to Bay. She was always there. He'd quickly assumed that she lived there. After all she'd said that she was never going away. She never looked for any more than a shared love of the place and a joy in being there together. He'd puzzled about contacting her in term time or sending her letters but when he'd gently pressed her about her address or whether he could write to her she'd just smiled and said that things were best left as they were.

'The way things are, there are no complications and we make no demands on each other. I'm happy with that if you are?'

Michael knew that he'd made a mess of one relationship by running into it in a headstrong manner and he knew that Sara had escaped from a disturbing marriage and so for the present he was quite happy to know that whenever he returned to Bay he'd have a close friend at hand to share everything with.

There were one or two things that puzzled him. The first was that she always seemed to find him wherever he was or she arranged that he would bump into her after he'd set out. The other was that she preferred the open air and could seldom be tempted into tea rooms, bookshops or pubs. On the few occasions that they did go into a pub or bookshop, she seemed relieved to escape and glad to be out again in the fresh air. Once, when in a bookshop together one rainy afternoon, he'd collected some strange glances and wondered why they should attract such attention.

The friendship was a deep platonic one. They had never progressed to intimacy as his first relationship had. In fact although they had never yet clasped hands, their minds and hearts had certainly seemed closer than any other union he'd experienced. There was a shared joy, a warmth of the heart and a lightness and awareness that heightened their shared hours. It was mutual he knew. He felt a little guilty that he was not giving more but was assured that she wanted no more from the friendship.

Was it right that he should expect her to be there for him whenever he wanted? he mused. But then, she usually found him. There was a lecturer he knew at one of the colleges who had a girlfriend he met every summer in the same resort. No questions were asked, they both just turned up regularly over the years. It went on for decades. But then this was different. Sara was not so much a girlfriend as a soul mate and he would be devastated if he thought he couldn't see her from one year to the next.

And so it went on. It went on because the players in the drama wanted it to. It was as simple as that. Later, when Michael began to understand what was happening it was too late. He still wanted it to go on.

It was the painting that started the process. Michael had been in Bay for about a week during a summer of the mid seventies when he had cause to walk up bank to collect his car from the top car park. He'd done this dozens of times and there was nothing out of the ordinary about that. On this occasion however, he happened to glance into the window of one of the shops and was brought up sharp. There in the corner, neatly framed, was a portrait of a girl. It was Sara. She was seated on the cliff top and was looking out to sea. The pose alone told him it was her. He crossed over and stared at the picture. It was a water-colour, delicately done and signed at the bottom left corner. Whoever had painted it must have met Sara because it was so amazingly true to life. It was a beautiful picture and so fetching it set his heart racing. Of course he had to have it so he went into the shop hoping that no-one else had set their heart on it.
Waiting in a queue of children was torment. At last his turn came.

'The painting in the window!' he blurted.
There was only one water-colour among the prints and framed memorabilia and the lady in the shop seemed to know just which one it was.

'You mean the painting of the girl?'

'Yes!'

'We only decided to put it out this morning. We've had it in store for a number of years. The gentleman who commissioned it never came back for it.'

'What can you tell me about it?' pressed Michael.

'As I said, it was commissioned a number of years ago by a gentleman who was staying here. It was a portrait of his wife to be and she was to get it on her wedding day. Only he never came back for it. Never paid for it either.'

'Who painted it?'

'A lady called Caroline Bebington, a prominent and much sought after portraitist and animal painter. She is well known nationally and has had several acclaimed exhibitions. I think she did the brochures for Rolls Royce cars too. She was on holiday here and painted one or two local scenes which we framed. The gentleman saw her work and asked her to paint his fiancee. As you can see, she did.'

'Can I have a look at it?'

'Certainly you can.'

Michael looked long and hard at the picture. Knowing Sara, he felt it was a brilliant likeness. Yes, he just had to have it. Of course Sara must have known it existed because she posed for it. But then she'd never seen the final picture if it was never collected.

'How much do you want for it?' asked Michael

'It will have to be fifty five pounds, that includes the framing of course. It's a bit expensive but then the artist is well known.'

'I'll take it please,' said Michael quickly, 'and could you look up the name of the gentleman concerned?'

'It'll take a few minutes. I'll have to look up the old stock books.'

'That's fine,' said Michael, 'and thanks.'

After what seemed an age, she returned with a folder crammed with papers, slips, documents, bills and invoices. On the cover was a faded and scuffed square of paper bearing the legend "1946 - 1962".

'This is Dad's business record. He put everthing in here. It looks a bit untidy but it's in strict date order and everything is ticked off meticulously.'

As she thumbed back through the years, Michael noticed handwritten notes and newspaper clippings attached to various bills and receipts. It seemed quite a comprehensive record. At last she stopped and looked up.

'It's longer ago than I thought, Look, "July 18th 1957, Mr P. Sanderson. To collect commissioned portrait, framed. No deposit." '

Michael looked at the picture again. It might have been painted yesterday. It was as fresh and crisp as a new banknote.

'It looks brand new to me. Are you sure it's that old?'

'Oh yes. It was wrapped up in a parcel for travelling and has been in the storeroom. I think that's why it was left for so long. No-one remembered it was there.'

Michael continued. 'The girl in the picture, Sara, she lives in the village. She'll be up and down the Bank regularly. I expect you've seen her or even know her.'

'I don't think so. I know most of the folk who live here. I was born here myself and I don't recognise her. Besides, I'm sure they were visitors not residents.'

Michael let it go. There was the picture on the counter in front of him and he was going to buy it.

'One more question. This Sanderson fellow, did he ever enquire about the picture? Did he telephone or write?'

'No, now I come to think of it, there was a bit of a mystery at the time or shortly afterwards. Dad would have made a note of it.'

She opened the folder and quickly found the entry again. A strip of paper was attached to the back of the entry with a paper clip. 'Yes, here's something:

> "A man named Sanderson robbed a solicitor in Lincolnshire and ran off. His car was found abandoned on the main road near here but he was spotted leaving the country with his wife. Foreign police forces have been asked to look out for him."

'I seem to remember Dad saying that if it's the same fellow who's s'posed to come for that painting, we'll have to wait a long time. He was right. We put it by and forgot all about it until we cleared out the store-room this month. And, of course we've never been able to forward the money for it to the artist.'

'Where did she live?'

'North Staffordshire I think, but it will be in the book. Yes, here it is, "Longsdon, Leek, Staffordshire." But it's twenty years ago, she could be anywhere now.'

'Well now I've paid you, are you going to try and find where she is so you can pay her?'

'We'll give it a try.'

'If you come up with a result, I'd be glad to know.'

'Call in in a week or two and I'll let you know how we got on.'

'Thanks, I will.'

Michael counted out the money for the painting and left the shop. The lady smiled after him.

'What a truly marvellous stroke of luck,' he thought. 'I couldn't have wished for a more wonderful surprise.' The painting however posed more questions than he cared to answer. Firstly, she wasn't known in the town as a resident but he had known her here for a dozen years or more. Secondly, if she had gone abroad, she'd certainly returned and probably after their marriage failed. Thirdly, the picture showed Sara as he knew her. It was as if it had been painted yesterday. But according to the record in the shop ledger it was nearly twenty years ago and the girl in the picture would have turned forty.

The facts were such that the historian in him wanted to investigate the matter thoroughly and come to some concrete conclusions but the romantic boy in him didn't want the dream dissolved, his bubble pricked or his mind disturbed with such things as reality. He'd known, of course that some day he'd uncover more about Sara than she'd been able to tell him. There were so many ways in which she transcended the ordinary that there had to be something to be discovered. The sharp, blatant fact that she might not exist at all had occurred to him at the outset. He didn't care to think about it too often. If she was a projection from his own mind, what particular mental disorder was he suffering from?

Michael decided that he would show the picture to Sara and gauge her reactions. If she admitted she was the subject then the time had come for them to look at the problem of the missing years and the wonder of their ongoing meetings.

Abandoning his ideas for the day, Michael tucked the picture under his arm and set off down bank, down New Road and on down the slip. Resolutely he turned right along the beach toward Mill Beck. It was time to confront his fears. Of course he was aware of the possible consequences. He was only amazed that the dream had gone on for so long. He met up with her half way to Mill Beck. She was sitting on a largish stone close under the fractured, tumbling cliff and waiting for him. She smiled up at him. He was framing the questions in his mind.

Pulling the picture from under his arm, he tore off the brown paper wrapping and thrust it towards her.

'This is you, isn't it?' he said quietly.

Sara looked long at the picture.

'So she painted it after all. She made the sketches for it during an afternoon here in Bay when Peter decided to have a day to himself. We came here you know, just before we married. It all seems so long ago.'

She smiled again, a little sadly.

'I wondered how you'd react when you discovered the facts. I thought you'd realised some time ago. We've met for years and you never asked the direct questions and I never volunteered any answers. You've respected my silence and my ways and I've felt free to grow and to value the breadth of your friendship. You know now, don't you?'

Michael sank down beside her.

'Not all of it. It's the shock when I realise that you've not changed at all, not caught in time as I am. Yes, I knew something was unusual, out of the ordinary, but I didn't want to face it. I confess I liked things as they were, as they are.'

'To you I've not changed but if I were still alive, I'd be over forty now and would look different from this!'

Michael nodded soberly.

'At first I thought that everyone could see me but then I realised it was only a few. I was thrilled to discover that you could see me. Remember when you were picking up pebbles? You should have seen your face! You knew didn't you? Yet you said nothing and behaved as if we had a regular friendship. I liked you for that.'

Michael rummaged for words.

'I think that I needed a friendship too.'

Sara twisted her head round and looked him in the eye.

'I've found you honest and gentle where before I found deceit and hurt. I found you warm and open where before I found stony coldness. I found your heart was much like mine, without selfishness or guile.'

She leaned back and put her head on one side.

'You did realise didn't you? she persisted.

'Well, not at first, but subconsciously I suppose I did. I just avoided asking the questions until the picture told me I had to face up to it.'

'I'll tell you everything if you like. I still need a bit longer. I don't know how long. Time is a strange thing for me, the last years have flashed by and I've noticed the changes around me and yet in many ways I'm still caught up with my reasons for being here. You should get involved with your world, you can't escape for ever on these beaches. I've learned that. Find a person you can cling to, walk with and share with.'

Michael thought he had all he needed. He didn't want things to change.

'If this situation has allowed us both to grow and to find peace, why shouldn't it go on?' insisted Michael.

'That's the point, Michael,' she went on, 'we are both growing in maturity and understanding and that changes things.'

'I'd rather go on as now,' he said solemnly.

'Yes, I know, at times so would I but the years are adding to you and I am still caught. We could have years or months but don't be too surprised if one summer I'm not here any longer. I don't know if I am mistress of the drama. You must find a companion of your own, someone bright and sensitive as you are.'

She smiled encouragingly, then went on seriously.

'This has already developed further that it ought. Initially I couldn't rest, was angry, hurt and lost but here I found my peace and a rhythm that healed. I needed to know that there were still people like you in the world and so I experimented and you saw me.'

'But we've shared so much,' said Michael.

'Not in a normal way,' Sara shook her head. 'Not as it should be. It could never be like that for us. Some would say that I'm a figment of your imagination or a projection of your subconscious in order to create the partner that could never hurt you. Perhaps I am. Think about it!'

'No, the picture tells me that you are, you were real.'

'Yes, but a matter of months after it was painted, I ceased to be a part of your world. I chose to end it, out there, where you nearly smashed up that boat! You must go on and look for the right one.'

Michael sighed.
Sara rose to her feet.

'Look, I only exist in your consciousness for a few fleeting hours each year. The energy I draw on is pure emotion and thanks to you I'm approaching the time when I'll be able to leave all this, even the places and the person I've come to love. I needed you. I needed the place and the time to heal. I suppose I used you, needed you to see me and help me to see the world afresh without hurt, clean, new, washed like the beach after a full tide.'

'Have I been the only one to see you? queried Michael.

'Lots of children see me. Few adults can. They are too fixed in their own realities. But I've met lots of children here, happy, inquisitive, open and straightforward. They don't challenge with a set of rules. There's more room in their minds and hearts for the possibilities. One lonely little girl told me her life's story over a fortnight. I think she went home feeling much better.'

Michael stood up and together they turned along the beach. A lazy tide was slipping back into the sea and the day was still.

'What happened after you ran away with your husband?' Michael probed gently.

'I didn't.' Sara took a deep breath. 'He ran off with someone else and all the money in the holding account from the solicitors where we worked. Everyone thought we'd run off together and that the car being left up here was a red herring to put the police off the scent. In fact I drove the car here on my last night. I've not been able to share this with anyone. I think I still have a need to set the record straight and to let those that care know what actually happened.'

'I'd like to help,' said Michael.

'I know you would. Now things are out in the open, there's a lot you can do. My mother is still alive and I'd like her to learn the facts. Suicide is a harsh idea to impart and she will need your support. As for Peter, he's long forgotten me and is married for the third time, I believe.'

Michael now felt up to it. His long apprenticeship of teetering on the brink of full comprehension had at last brought him to accept with the sixteenth century scholar Noel Taillepied, that "there are verily and indeed Spirits and Phantoms which sometimes appear to men." He'd met a ghost! Put like that it sounded fantastic but put another way, he'd experienced a conscious encounter with someone who had passed over, it didn't sound so bad. Was it solely the power of emotion that generated the ability to transcend the death experience or was it an overriding need to tell someone what had happened, to share the trauma or to obtain some relief? In this case years had gone by since the tragic drowning and Sara had been content to discover a new harmony from the familiar beachscape and from a fresh relationship. She'd needed time, peace and gentle encouragement after which she seemed to grow and mature. She was now looking at the loose ends.

He'd not done much reading about ghosts but he'd discovered that the genuine ghost always seemed to be looking for help to put something right, for reassurance or support. There was a very human element about them, not at all how fiction would portray them. He'd heard of several unquiet ghosts that had sought the proper rites and dignity of a funeral after which they had been happy to move on. Sara now appeared more or less settled and ready to tidy up the details. She'd come to terms with her traumatic passing and had left the hurt behind. If she wanted him to reassure her mother, he would be happy to do so. Funny thing was, while he was with her, she looked as solid as anyone else and he was prompted to ask himself whether he was the victim of an elaborate hoax and his spook a spoof!

'This has all happened,' he posed, 'our meeting, our on-going dialogue, our friendship?'

'Oh yes, all too true I'm afraid. I see I'll have to give you some kind of proof and talk you through some of the details. Now, distance and time are no problem for me so after you leave me here, I'll stay behind and then meet you at the top of the slip.'

Michael frowned.

'No, I can't be in two places at the same time but I can place myself anywhere I wish at a moment's notice. You'll see.'

As they walked slowly on, Sara endeavoured to tell him about the nature of the state she found herself in. Michael listened but it still stretched his credulity. The whole situation was bizarre and yet there was a bond between them that he was loth to break. Their strange relationship had become very special to him despite its limitations.

'I ought to tell you that for the last year or two I haven't always been able to get your attention. You've missed me or I've not been able to get through. As you probably know there are lots of theories about spirits. We don't operate like the more common film-repeat type of experience. They are no more than emotionally-charged energy patterns caught in a particular environment or place that is able to support them. They are generated by humans under stress and will eventually fade. Similarly, the so-called crisis apparition, it is a mental thing between minds where those who are close or connected in some way catch a glimpse of the panic projection for a few brief seconds.'

'No, we are different. We have chosen to stay. We have the volition that other place-held ghosts lack. Not everyone can see us but we can find our way about in a flash, overcoming distance, time and effort. In a way life is faster, broader, fuller but we all have an eventual goal to which we are drawn. We can resist but as we mature we tend to accept our destiny and move on. There are others here in Bay; some have been active for hundreds of years, some in the town and some here, on the beach. Some still seek recognition long out of their time, some empathy and some, rites of passage. One or two have things left unsaid or undone that still need addressing.'

She went on. 'Now, I'm finding it harder to focus on Bay and to find you despite all that you have done for me. I often feel drawn away and get a glimpse of what I might be doing hereafter. So, as I said, I don't know how long we've got or if I'll be able to make full contact for much longer. It might be months or it might be years but I'm aware that there will be an end for you. There is still the matter of my mother to deal with. I've been to see her

but I can't break through the armour of her reality. You'll go for me won't you?'
Michael nodded.

'This is why I am urging you to take up an emotional life with someone in your world. If I discover anyone here that has a gentle heart, I'll let you know. You do understand don't you? There's no future in our friendship in your world and although it has gone on because we both wanted it to, it will have to come to an end one day.'

Michael nodded again but hoped in his heart of hearts that it would go on for a little while longer. He was intrigued to discover that there were others like Sara in the Bay area.

'Who else is here? I've never seen anyone else with your elusive qualities,' he smiled.

'Oh you have, you've just not realized they were of the spirit world! Do you remember two years ago here on the beach how you were feeling sorry for that little girl who was limping badly on one of the scaurs below the slip. She was soaking and you were on the verge of going to help her.'

'Why yes, she made it eventually. I saw her come up the beach. She...'

'Yes, she passed out of your sight. She was drowned in 1938 and still wants a proper service said for her. Her body, like mine, was washed out to sea and never found. Then you might have seen the old sailor. He's the oldest about here and is usually active in rough weather. He goes home to King Street where he's tried for ages to get someone to help him. He helped me on that morning long ago when I walked up this beach after my passing.

"You poor little maid, come 'ee 'ere." he said and he held me until I came to and discovered the dimensions of my new awareness. The drowned girl is Emma, if you were to pray for her it would help. The sailor is Andrew. He didn't drown, though listening to his story I can't think why he didn't. He died of old age in the town. He has unfinished business. He's a lovely old chap. Oh, and there's another sailor who walks up to Shell Hill after the fishing boats have been secured for the night.'

Michael remained silent.

'So let me show you a way of finding me if you can't visualise me or my signal isn't coming through. I might be close and you not be aware. You can use a stick or rod. Look, I'll show you.'

She stooped and indicated a sun-bleached twig.

'Here, use this. Snap off some of the branches until you have a rough L shape. This is crude, you can make yourself a better one when you get home. It can act as an indicator. Now, everyone, every sentient living entity has an energy field which is discernible to others. Mostly, we meet it unconsciously and hardly react to it but you can use a twig or rod to emphasise your awareness of the field. Try it on your colleagues or friends. It usually works a couple of feet out from the centre of the body. Watch me and copy me.'

Sara held her hand out, her fingers lightly folded as if the twig was in the palm of her hand with the branch projecting before her. She moved slowly towards Michael and as she did so, the twig twisted in his hand.

'There,' she said, 'see it move. You've picked up my energy. So, hold the rod thus, walk or move towards the person in question and the rod will react when you come up against the energy field. It's just that the body's finely tuned electrical system can detect other fields of energy. Try it near pylons, they are the heavyweights of the energy world! Now the magic bit is that it works for us as well as the living so if you want to establish whether or not a spirit is present, dowse for us and you'll get the same reaction as for the living, positive proof that someone is there.'

'Is this some kind of magic then?' queried Michael in disbelief.

'No, it's called dowsing, folk use it for finding water or minerals. You can use it for finding the likes of us!'

'What else will it do?'

'You're the scholar, look it up. There's lots of books about. Anyone can do it but few will be using it for the purpose I've told you about.'

Michael nodded. 'I will. We're not short of books in Oxford!'

'Don't forget, the brain is the receptor of all stimuli, data and signals in proximity to the body, the senses are the means whereby you channel them. Data sometimes gets to the brain without the usual sensory stimuli, then, of course, the only way in which you can say that you've received data is to say you've seen, felt or heard it when it hasn't been any of those channels responsible. You don't see me via your eyes, you only think you do. I come through to your brain and you receive me.That's why you see me in my fifties clothes, they are part of the data package I signal. The data is stable, like a signature. We can't be measured, photographed or recorded because we don't exist outside the receiver's head. It makes us laugh when these ghost hunting characters set off with their equipment to catch physical phenomena when, if they were sensitive, they could catch it all.'

'Where does the dowsing come in? Tell me again.'

'The dowsing rod is simply an amplifier. It allows you to have evidence of what you cannot immediately see. It is a disciplined, active interrogative, a questioning using the whole body as an instrument. Pose the question and the body's full awareness comes into play and the rod or stick indicates the result for you. We are all far more sensitive that we are aware. Some more than others. We just don't use these gifts and so they die in us.'

'I follow you.'

'Now remember, if you can't see me and you have an feeling that I'm around, dowse for me. Be specific. Ask a direct question. You'll soon catch on. It's easy enough.' Sara stopped and Michael dropped the twig on the sand.

'You'll make a better one out of a piece of wire or brass rod. Small enough to go in your pocket. There are diagrams in books. Incidentally, you don't hear me with your ears either. My voice is going straight into your head. Someone close by might not hear anything at all. It's a lot to do with whether you are born with a good receiver. Some folk are able to receive a far wider range than the norm and others never will. You can't make rules for everyone. Science is only just beginning to allow for the things that should not happen if the universe is as the text books say.'

'Do you mean,' said Michael, 'that I've been talking to myself up and down this beach for years and in the town and in shops?'

'I'm afraid so, that is unless you happen to have been close to a sensitive person who might have seen us both. All our discourse, our exchanges our thoughts and feelings, even the most acute experiences have been going on in your head. I'm here all right but you'll never prove it!'

Michael thought about the odd glances he'd intercepted when deep in conversation with Sara. It wasn't as if it was an isolated incident. A lot of his time had been spent with Sara.

'They must have thought me a rather eccentric character.' he mused. 'Still, I know several lecturers who practice their delivery aloud.'

'Right,' said Sara, 'I hope you can remember all that. Dowsing can be our lifeline when I haven't the energy to get through. I shall leave you now but look out for me when you climb up the slip on your way back. I'll give you a wave!'

Michael looked at her. She was looking confident and buoyant, a half smile turning up the corners of her mouth. She was certainly a beauty and as he'd observed before, as solid as he was. This extended period of time they'd spent together had proved beneficial to both of them. Away from the hurts of the world, she had blossomed and seemed full of vitality whilst he had been free to pursue his researches and have the satisfaction of seeing them turned into books and degrees. His colleagues all seemed to collect both like stamps and he was no exception.

'Off you go! I'll see you tomorrow,' she grinned.

'Bully!' he returned.

He turned and set off with the sun at his back and gave himself the challenge to walk back on sand. It never worked but it was boyish fun and he'd never grown out of it. Sooner or later he'd have to clamber over rocks or scramble up shingle unless a heavy ground swell had shifted the beach about as it could do after severe weather. He looked back. She was still standing there. She raised her hand in the air and he waved back. The picture was still in his grasp and he found it difficult to wait until he got back when he could take a really good look at it. Now things were changing, it was doubly valuable and he'd treasure it always.

'What a day!' he thought. 'First the picture, then the confrontation with Sara followed by her amazing introduction to dowsing and her lecture on the other world. I can barely take it all in. Still, I can look it all up in the library when I get access to a decent one.'

He turned around again and found the high ground and the cliffs in shadow. The light was picking out distant Ravenscar and the tide had turned. A tiny figure was still standing at the foot of the cliffs waving. He waved back. He felt strangely privileged and sought for more words to frame the story. Why was it always words with him? Why did he find it necessary to frame events and clothe them with words. He could only think that it must be his academic training. His mind just worked that way.

And why this beach,
These cliffs, high lifting
The long cloud shadows
Across the scaurs.

Why this beach,
Low, lias lined,
Flung with shingled sand
And shouting water
Where sky-filled pools
Reflect the passing of your years.

Your choice Sara, your Bay,
Stone-crafted
For the commerce of your way.

Another fifteen minutes saw him nearing the slip. The ponies were there and a crowd of holiday-makers were sitting on and around the base of Beacholme. An ice-cream man was ringing a bell and several small children were damming the stream that issued at the side of the cobbled slipway. He felt tired. The hot sand and even hotter sun had sucked him dry and so he thought that if the Bay Hotel was open, he'd pop in for a pint. 'Lovely thought!'

He looked up. There standing by the railings looking down at him was Sara. Michael looked way back down the beach, then up at the top of the slip. She raised a hand and slipped away.

THE WRATH
THE WRATH
OF GOD
Gilman '98.

CHAPTER ELEVEN

Dick awoke just after ten feeling refreshed. Within the hour he was up, washed, breakfasted and eager to tell Annie about the adventures of the night. Sylvia had been first down, noticing Dick snoring not so quietly by the embers of the fire. She wondered what he'd been up to. Her mind was on her day, a day off from the bookshop when she would go to Whitby for lunch and a heart to heart with her friend Bess. There was an exhibition on at the Pannett Gallery and she didn't want to miss it. By nine-o-clock she'd departed.

Annie stirred just after ten and deliberately indulged herself in her surroundings. It was so easy to let the intervening years flee away and imagine herself a child again. She loved this room. It was quiet in the cottage and she'd been unaware of the screaming gulls that had choired the town since first light.

'Annie!' called Dick. 'Are you staying up there all day?'

'Coming!'

Annie thought of a traditional breakfast and wondered if her father had gone to such lengths. She'd always enjoyed her grub, in fact her father had likened her to Desperate Dan and his passion for cow pies.

'It's on the table!' he intoned.

Annie shot out of bed and tumbled down the stairs, a large grin of expectation on her face. There on the table was a breakfast to be reckoned with.

'A full Naval breakfast,' he announced, 'just like the old days.'

Annie pulled up a chair and tucked in.

'Super, Dad. Bay always gives me an appetite.'

'Now,' Dick enjoined. 'Let me tell you about last night.'

'Go on!'

'Well, I met this Andrew who used to live here and he spent the entire evening telling me all about his adventures at sea in Elizabeth's reign. I could hardly get a word in edgeways!'

'So this was his house?'

'Yes. He told me that he wanted me to do something for him but didn't finish.'

'What did you think of the experience,' pressed Annie, 'seeing him there and understanding what he was trying to say to you?'

'It was literally out of this world. I would never have believed it had I not seen it with my own eyes. He seemed so real. He was a sailor all right. He'd been there, in battle and in gales. What an amazing man! I wonder what he wants?'

'We'll have to wait and see. By his habits it looks as if we'll have to wait until the next high wind or rough sea.'

'I can hardly grasp it. I've heard him for years but not seen him until now. Do you think I dreamed it all?'

'No.' Annie shook her head. 'There was a definite presence here last night.'

'Is this sort of thing unusual?' enquired Dick.

'It's far more prevalent than is widely acknowledged. There are lots of ghosts about, after all they are as human as you and me. generated by humans and for the purpose of gaining help. Mostly their needs can be easily satisfied and then they can rest.'

'I wonder what Andrew wants and why he's been trying for so long?'

'We shan't have long to wait. As the year goes on, there'll be plenty of heavy weather about.'

Dick nodded. 'When you've done, we'll take a turn up the beach and I can fill you in on the details of last night.'

Annie polished off her breakfast. What a luxury it was not to have to cook it for herself. On her own she seldom bothered but when, more usually, the boys were at home she made sure that they didn't go hungry and made do with the left-overs.

'That was super, Dad!'

'Come along then. Leave the washing up for now. I'm bursting to tell you about Andrew.'

Pulling their coats on, for it was still quite cool after the turbulent night's aquatic display, they turned down King Street and made for the beach, streaming clean and beginning to haze as the morning sun tackled the edges of the retreating tide. During their walk Dick carefully recounted all that he had heard and understood.

'It was as if Andrew had it all bottled up and just needed the opportunity to spill it all out.'

'Could you understand everything he said?'

'Well, there were several words I didn't get but I could understand the gist of it all. They were pretty violent times to live in!'

'But then, so were your service years,' persisted Annie.

'Yes, but I'd rather be on a corvette with a four inch gun than an Elizabethan sailing ship armed with cannon.'

'There's not much difference from what I see of it, it's still ship against ship and the better one wins whatever the period.'

'I wonder what Andrew wants? Perhaps he'll come out with it next time.'

'I'd very much like to be there next time if, of course, I'm still here in Bay. I might not be able to see anything but I could dowse to confirm his arrival.'

'I was thinking that we could share this experience with Michael. He's a dowser and if what folk say about him is true, he's seen things too. I've never approached him but as you are here, we might get a wider insight into the matter.'

'That would be interesting. If we spot him this morning we could ask him.'

However there was no sight of Michael, the beach was clear and they followed along the familiar sandways and rocky stepping stones as far as Mill Beck. Above, the sky was beginning to clear and the sun grew warmer by the hour. By midday the far shouting sea had felt slack water and was beginning to surge once again up the shore, its long sea fingers seeking between the dried out, shell-encrusted scaurs.

Dick enjoyed the company of his daughter. It was a long time since they could wander along the beach together exchanging thoughts and sharing problems. This episode of Andrew had been brewing for decades and although it stretched and puzzled him it was, in some strange way, a relief to get it out into the open. He'd never thought of himself as a believer in ghosts and yet it was hard to dismiss the impact of the previous evening's entertainment. He was relieved that Annie was at hand as she seemed to take these things in her stride.

Annie felt refreshed, eager and confident. She relished the idea of getting to the bottom of the mystery and of sharing the adventure with Michael. She had, of course, glimpsed him about the town over the years but he'd posed a reclusive figure and she'd never felt the necessity to introduce herself. Now it was different, she had been introduced and there appeared to be a sharing of interests. She wondered about his life and why he appeared to be so attached to Bay.

They strolled on, under the higher and straighter range of cliff that imposed itself after the unstable rubble of the boulder clay that ran back into Bay. Piles of sharp-faced rock lay directly under the edge proving, if one needed proof, that even these massive bulwarks were vulnerable to the incessant attack of the sea. They both felt the wariness that came from long hours of beach walking and kept well out from the base. Even on the stillest day one could hear the pitter patter of tiny stones skittering down the steep slopes.

Dick looked at his watch.

'Might just be time for a pint before lunch,' he smiled. 'I won't be getting you into bad habits will I?'

Within half an hour they were stepping up the steep ledge at the base of the slip and looking forward to a cool pint. They stepped aside to allow the tractor room to chunter noisily past with a double-ender in tow. Gaining the Dock they were about to turn into the Bay when Dick noticed the spare figure of Michael standing half obscured by visitors at the rail. He touched Annie's arm.

'Look, there's Michael.'

'He looks preoccupied,' returned Annie. 'Do you think we ought to bother him?'

'Oh, he won't mind. He always walks about with a serious expression or talking to himself but that doesn't mean he's anti-social. I'll fetch him!'

Dick strode over, passing between several couples who were sitting and standing talking and drinking.

'Michael!'

'Hello, Dick.'

'Come on now, you turned us down yesterday, come and meet my daughter Annie. Like you she's a keen dowser.'

Michael jerked awake.

'Sorry, I was miles away. Yes, I'd be delighted.'

The two of them made their way toward the steps where Annie was waiting.

Once settled with their pints in the window, Michael turned straightway to Annie.

'Dick tells me that you are a dowser.'

'Yes, I've dowsed for a number of years now and covered most aspects of it.'

'Have you ever done map-dowsing?' asked Michael.

'Yes, I helped to discover the whereabouts of a body once. That was quite exciting. Oh, and I've used it several times to find the location of old wells and drains. The usual things.'

'I used it here on the beach when it was imperative to find a missing child. It worked well for me then. Have you ever used dowsing to find lost or missing articles?'

'Yes, and dowsing to discover whether or not there are any presences about or ghosts as most folk would call them.'

Michael leaned across the table.

'Can you detect spirits?' he asked earnestly.

'That's exactly why we are talking to you now,' inserted Dick. 'We've got a classic ghost in the cottage and last night we made contact for the first time. Kept me up all night!'

'Tell me.'

'Well, I've been hearing things for a long time but last night discovered that we have a very real presence, if you can call a ghost real. It was an old sailor. Annie here dowsed for him and confirmed that she could detect him also. Seems that he has a message for me as I am living in the house that he used to live in.'

'What was the message?'

'Well that's it, he hasn't given it to me yet but he promised to tell me later. We thought, as you have an interest in dowsing you'd like to come along and join us when he decides to give us the message.'

'Count me in please. I'd be most interested. You see, I've had some extraordinary experiences where spirits are concerned. It's a relief to find someone else who doesn't think I'm completely loony.'

Annie added, 'You'd be most welcome. Where are you staying at the moment? One of us could come over and give you a knock, that is if we don't bump into you in the town.'

Michael lowered his voice.

'Did you actually see this character last night?'

'As clearly as I see you now, that is until just after dawn when he just faded away. In fact I saw him, heard him and thought I could detect the odour of rope and tar about him.'

Michael nodded.

'I believe you wholeheartedly. I've had a similar experience myself right here in Bay. In fact I'd hazard a guess that your mariner's name is Andrew. Am I right?'

Dick and Annie looked surprised.

'I heard about Andrew and others that are still here many years ago when I was in contact with someone. It's a long story.'

'Do you see ghosts then?' asked Annie.

'At first I never believed I had that ability but subsequent experience told me that I have. Additional research has encouraged me to believe that there are a considerable number of people who can see ghosts but accept them as part of reality. Unless they stand out or slowly fade in front of you, how do you know that you haven't seen lots during a lifetime?'

'I don't see them but am particularly sensitive to their energy fields. I can dowse them.'

'As I can now,' replied Michael. 'When I find it increasingly difficult to pick up a visual signal from a particular subject, I switch to dowsing for the personal energy pattern and can get a positive reaction. Communication takes longer but you get there in the end.'

Dick sat back and shook his head. He knew that Michael had an interest in dowsing but he had no idea that the scope was so wide or that it encompassed the ground usually associated with mediums and claivoyants. He'd always steered clear of such characters as they had such a bad press and were seldom taken seriously. He took a long drink and shuffled back in his seat. Here he was talking about contacting a ghost in his own house and in the company of folk who did this regularly. It was still a novelty and he would have to be careful who knew about it. He wondered how Sylvia would react with her down-to-earth appraisal of all things paranormal. She could hardly call this a myth.

By now, Michael and Annie had their heads together and were discussing the many books and papers that attempted to explain what a ghost was. Starting with the French and German scholars of the sixteenth century right up to Charles Lindley, Viscount Halifax, M.R James, T. C. Lethbridge and Ian Wilson, they began to tease out their favourite descriptions and definitions.

'We have this group back at home,' Annie continued, 'in which there are representatives of all the inquisitive disciplines. There are dowsers, seers, mediums, healers and many allied talents so that it is possible to bring skills and learning together for co-operative and collaborative investigations. It's probably the biggest group in the country and attracts folk from five counties. So, for instance, if we have a report that a particular householder has asked for help, we can send a team who are able to offer different skills yet work to a common end.'

'And do you go with them, Annie?'

'On many occasions. Yes.'

'I think we'll have to continue this conversation later. There's too much to talk about right here.'

Dick looked at his watch.

'Do you two know what the bloody time is?' he demanded. 'We've been here over an hour. I'm off home to get some lunch.'

He smiled at Annie.

'You stay on here if you like. You can catch up with me later. Bye, Michael.'

Michael raised a hand and turned to Annie.

'It's strange that we should get to know each other now. I was told that a sensitive person was in the town but never realised it was you. I've seen you in Bay before but never took the initiative to say hello. Well, to tell the truth, I was preoccupied with my own ghostly experience which went on for decades.'

Annie smiled.

'Yes, I've seen you too over the years. In the early days I seem to recall you on the beach sometimes with a younger girl and sometimes alone. Later you always appeared to have your head in a book or be rehearsing some speech or other!'

'Stop there!' Michael put his hand on Annie's arm. 'I thought you said that you were not a seer, that you couldn't see ghosts but rather sensed them.'

'That's right. To my knowledge I've never seen one but I've certainly dowsed dozens!'

'But you said just now that you saw me on the beach years ago with a young girl.'

'So?'

'Then you have seen a ghost. The girl I met here in Bay and in fact met regularly in the town does not belong to this world. No-one to my knowledge has seen her but me. What is more, it was she who told me about Andrew and others who are still active in Bay.'
Michael looked earnestly at Annie.

'The story is fantastic. I don't believe that anyone but you would believe it. Will you listen to it?'
Annie nodded.

'Sara, for that is her name, burst into my consciousness during one summer in the early sixties. At first I thought she was as alive as you and I but as the number of meetings increased I realised that she was too elusive to belong to my reality. Elusive is probably the best word to use in the context because it was some time before I realised that she dictated the time and place of each meeting and what I had put down to chance in the early days was not the case. I only found her when she wanted me to. I was a strange subject for her to chose for I am a scholar and one used to probing for the truth or the nearest one can get to it from the evidence in hand. We met each summer and as we grew to relax in each other's company I learned of her background and of her love for Bay. That was the mainstay of her power to exist. Matters came to a head when, after nearly twenty years of meeting her in the town and on the beach, I found a picture of her in one of the shops and showed it to her. It turned out that it was painted the year before she died when she was here on holiday with the man who betrayed her. She then told me the full story. She also confided that she feared that the impetus that had allowed her to stay in Bay was slowly fading and that she didn't know how much longer she might be able to remain in contact. As it turned out, we went on meeting for a further fifteen years during which she never altered one jot. In the last couple of years the meetings were not visual but only through dowsing. She was such a lovely girl, bright, warm and trusting and needed the time to find her peace and a measure of balance before moving on. She's gone now, though I can't overcome the habit of a lifetime and stop looking up the beach for a glimpse of her. Before she went she told me I'd meet someone here in Bay who would be of like mind.'

'When was the last meeting?' asked Annie.

'Last summer. I was well up the beach when I felt she was close. I looked out for her but the beach was empty. Then I realised that I might dowse for her and so I sat down and asked whether or not she was near. The answer was yes. She told me that she was happy and that she hoped I would find the right partner. She ended by thanking me for my encouraging friendship and love. Then she left me and no amount of dowsing would restore her. Looking back, she taught me a great deal of which the most important was that empathy, compassion and love were the keys that could release the most obdurate spirits and that all ghosts were on a pathway to harmony and peace but could do with a helping thought or prayer.'

Annie agreed.

'Yes, the latest books published on the subject stress that ghosts are very human and are not the monsters of popular fiction. Ian Wilson, for instance, makes a plea for compassion and understanding with a view to helping them through their crises or difficulties.'

'What did she say about Andrew?'

'It was some years ago now, but she was telling me about some of the other spirits in Bay and that Andrew was probably the oldest of them all. She said he had unfinished business in the town and had become very frustrated because he had, so far, not been able to make any contact or progress. She also said that he was a lovely old chap who had helped her in her crisis.'

'Well, we should be able to make contact soon. Dick will be able to see him and we should be able to dowse him. Who knows, you might be lucky enough to see him too.'

They were both sitting with empty glasses and probably wouldn't have noticed had not a couple sat opposite them and moved their glasses out of the way. Michael straightened and leaned back from his position dominating the table.

'How thoughtless of me,' he exclaimed. 'Let me get you another one.'

He eased out of his seat and took up the glasses.

'Same again?'

'Yes please.'

As he went up to the corner bar Annie followed him with her eyes. He seemed ingenuous, intuitive and interesting. He had the rare combination of practiced intelligence and sensitivity which was immediately apparent once one had broken the ice and discarded the image of the distant academic. It would be stimulating to get to know him better. In fact she looked forward to it.

Michael returned with the beer overflowing his fingers. He met her gaze, smiled, put the beer down and somewhat self-consciously wiped his hands on his trousers.

'Cheers!'

'Here's to Andrew's secret!.'

'Yes, I'm really looking forward to that.'

Annie was keen to return to the subject of Sara.

'During your long conversations with Sara, when she referred to other presences here in Bay did she mention a local man who lingered about the Dock and at the bottom of Tyson's Steps, probably a pipe smoker?'

'I don't think so. She talked about a little girl who was drowned off the scaurs and a house where she herself feared to go for the strength of evil and malevolence in the basement.'

'Where was that?' queried Annie.

'Sara wouldn't say. She stressed that there were places best left alone and that if I should find this place by accident or report I shouldn't attempt to discover the reasons. She said that it took a lifetime of anger to build up such power and that it would take several lifetimes to dispel it. The living could only be harmed.'

Michael went on.

'I think I know which place she meant now. I was asked by an old friend for my opinion of the house and visited it once. It's not a place you'd like to spend the night in. I've dowsed it since and there's a very strong presence there. I've taken Sara's advice and not probed further.'

'Lucky you had the warning, There are some ghosts that resist even the strongest human attempts to move them on. I've known some that resist prayers, masses and even exorcisms, they're just too obdurate or fixed in their purpose. With some, it's fear and with others it's sheer dogged resolve to achieve something. Luckily not all are like this and are receptive to offers of help. Were there any more?'

'Yes, Sara did mention one particular girl still trying to attract attention in one of the cottages just off the Bank. Apparently she's tried every kind of mischief and naughtiness but has failed to find a listener. On the last occasion she frightened a workman out of the house and was really upset not to make contact.'

Michael thought that this was something that they could perhaps tackle together. They seemed to have arrived at the same stage of understanding and experience where the paranormal was concerned. Neither thought the other at all unusual. It was easier for Annie, she belonged to a large group of open minded practitioners but for Michael it was the realization that here was another person with experience of the paranormal to match his own and that he was by no means alone in his gifts. Apart from that Michael felt somewhat unnerved. He discovered a self-consciousness and felt the stirrings of some very old feelings that he though had been dormant for ages. He felt eager yet vulnerable, light hearted yet serious. It dawned on him that he was finding this lady a very attractive person indeed. There was no need to press for a further meeting. She'd already indicated that he was welcome to join in their rendezvous with Andrew.

He couldn't wait.

"The Bartholomew of Exeter"
J.G.
'98

CHAPTER TWELVE

It was several days before the weather promised another early autumnal blow. Dick had been anxiously watching the weather forecasts on the television and looking at the isobars on the screen with an old professional interest.

On the morning before the day Annie was due to go back, things looked promising, a strong northerly air-stream seemed certain to strengthen right down the east coast gusting up to thirty or forty miles an hour. It wasn't a storm but it was the next best thing and, if Dick's memory was accurate, it should be sufficient to prompt Andrew.

Soon after eight o'clock and almost without warning a cold north-easterly squall swept into Bay in a welter of white water, first smothering the scaurs and then boiling up the beach and flinging up clouds of salt-weighted spray that was whipped shorewards by the sheer aggression behind it. Far from subsiding or moderating as was forecast, the squall settled into a bludgeoning, battering roar where it was hard to distinguish between the wind's constant ragged base and the fluctuating insistence of the rising tide. It was these unpredictable north-easters that often disturbed the otherwise sheltered waters of the bay.

Blustering westerlies were mostly swept far overhead as they lifted over the bulk of the moor and descended far out to feather the horizon. Local weather patterns could vary considerably from the regional forecasts and often Bay would enjoy a sheltered sunny day when conditions only ten miles away were far from comfortable. The north-easterlies were the problem. Trapped in the bay and funnelled between the scaurs they quickly established a nasty short sea that developed high rollers and a wicked undertow as the wind and the tide joined for the flood and fought on the ebb.

'What do you think?' queried Annie as she pushed the door to behind her.

Dick looked up. 'I think you'd better warn Michael to stand by for tonight. A bit of a blow was forecast but this is more like a December gale than an autumn one. I think it will last for a good few hours if my experience is anything to go by.'

'Is Mum in?'

'She's in the kitchen making some supper. I haven't told her about any of this.'

'Let's wait and see if anything happens. If it does, we'll have something extraordinary to tell . We can judge that later.'

Dick pursed his lips. 'I don't like keeping her in the dark but I'd feel such an idiot if it all turned out to be a lot of nonsense.'

'My dowsing definitely confirmed a presence here. You were certainly not dreaming.'

'What if I was, and you just picked up on my thought patterns?'

Annie spoke convincingly. 'I'm not often wrong about these things, Dad. I'll walk over and leave a message for Michael to join us after nine or when he can make it.'

By ten o'clock the streets had emptied. There were not even the few intrepid visitors daring the top of the slip to brave the perpetual stream of fine spume that lashed into the base of the old coastguard station and deflected into the Dock. The sky, moonlightened through the ever-moving, thickening layers of dense cloud, broke into isolated swirling pools of brilliance where it seemed to boil as the incoming colder air tore into the slow-rising village dusk. Seldom had a storm risen so quickly or been so insistently maintained. It promised to be a fearful night. High on Fisherhead a dog howled, its voice distorted and carried away on the wind.

Cosy in the cottage, Dick, Sylvia and Annie enjoyed a quiet supper. Quiet because Dick seemed preoccupied and failed to oversee the conversation with his usual aplomb. Sylvia twice mentioned a book she had found and would have filled in the details but no-one asked her. Before clearing away, she switched the tape-recorder on and allowed an orchestra to fill the room with a concert that although familiar, failed to hold or excite as it might have done on another evening. She put it down to the change in the weather and after taking the dishes out to the kitchen, settled down with the book in question and was soon miles away. Annie smiled at Dick and slipped out, returning within minutes to confirm that the message had been delivered.

For Sylvia the book proved to be the inevitable sleeping potion and with a nod and a smile, she tucked it under her arm and headed for the stairs.

'Don't you stay up too long or you'll fall asleep down here again.'

'Michael might drop in for a while,' added Dick.

'Give him my apologies, I'm going up. Good-night.'

Dick and Annie chorused their reply and, with a guilty look at the stairs, rearranged the chairs to form a semicircle about the fireplace. Just before eleven there came a tap at the door and Michael slipped in. In his hand he held a short brass dowsing rod set in bearings, shiny with use. Annie reached for hers and they settled to wait.

They were talking quietly about some of the older myths and beliefs of the coast and were just discussing the Hounds of Odin when Dick thought he caught the first indication of a sound that wasn't the wind.

'Gabble ratchets they're called here but in the south they are the Yeff hounds who scour the skies for souls. It's the ghostly hunt of the sky,' said Michael.

'Where does "gabble" come from?' asked Annie.

'Sometimes it's Gabriel but it all derives from the old word "gabares" which means death. They are the death dogs or the hell hounds that run to Odin's heels across the sky on such a night as this.'

Dick was not listening. He held his head up and the finger of his left hand was poised, not quite indicating that something was in the offing. The converstion died.

Annie took up her dowsing rod and concentrated. Dick sat up straight. Michael gasped and stared. Slowly, out of nothing developed the figure of a short, elderly seafarer standing before them. The two men soberly took in every detail. Annie spoke. 'He's here!'

Dick had seen him before and despite the barriers of reality or belief, felt strangely reassured. Michael felt animated and elated at the same time. Could this be the old seafarer that Sara had mentioned? He was sure it must be. He felt honoured to be included in the group.

Andrew smiled and looked about him.

'Got a bigger crew on board then! It's as well 'cos I've much to tell an' probably not much time to tell it. This gale'll blow itself out in an hour or two.'

The historian in Michael couldn't resist it.

'Did you see the Armada?' he blurted.

'Oh, by Our Lady! Yes, my son. Bless 'ee, yes. I were on the *Bartholomew* under young Nick Wright o' Exeter for the first engagements but left 'er injured when she re-victualled and re-ammunitioned in Weymouth. We joined Drake at Plymouth in mid July together with the *Rose* and the *Gift*. We was in action on the 23rd July off Portland an' I got struck by a splinter from one of the few balls that 'it us.'

Michael's mouth dropped open. Had anyone ever thought of interviewing a spirit from some great event of the past? He made a note to check out the details and to find out if those vessels really did take part in the fight against the Armada. His conversations with Sara had never moved much away from observations and personal details.

' 'Twas the October, two years on, when I were fit enough to ship again. I'd got back my old berth as Mate o' the *Wrath* an' we'd taken a small Spanish pinnace off the Isles. On All Souls Eve we was runnin' up the Bristol Channel an' ran into very 'eavy weather. Agin an ebb tide a sou-wester can be a bugger, especial across the Culvers. Early that evenin' we was struck by a particular tall sea. She were 'it by a squall that blew out 'er tops'ls an' plunged 'er fo'c'sle in deep. She never recovered, the 'uge weight of water below saw to that. Only five of us managed to 'scape drownin'.'

Andrew squatted down, his back to the stone of the chimney breast. He wrinkled up his eyes and his smile was not one of joy but recollection.

'Six hours we was in the water. Six hours, soaked, choked, dizzy an' 'alf drownded. The only thing that saved us was a length of broken tops'l yard.'

' 'Twere the sloop *Betsy* of Aberthaw that picked us up. She were out of Minehead for the Port of the Vale an' were ridin' out the gale under a steadyin' fores'l. She damn near run us down. A drover spotted us while strug-glin' to 'eave a drownded sheep over the side. They got us inboard wi' a lot o' cussin'. To brail up a long yarn we was set down on the stone jetty at Aberthaw. There we was, soaked, dirty, unshaven with nothing but the clothes we stood up in. It was Gentleman who saved us.

"You can pay me back later," 'e said, takin' off a money belt. We never knew 'e 'ad one! There were enough to take us all to Bristol. We parted company there.'

'I shipped for the London River an' there took passage aboard a barque wi' a cargo of yellow bricks for the Tees. We got up past the 'Umber an' then ran for Whitby an' the Esk wi' an onshore wind. This were a double dangerous time for me because I'd broke out all my share of the

Spanish voyages an' 'ad it with me in a 'pawlin bundle. 'Idden under a boat cloak, 'twere so 'eavy it made me sweat I can vouch! We ran in to Whitby over a shoal an' secured at the East Wharf. There weren't many big vessels there an' it seemed a poor place but for the fishin' boats of which there were dozens right across the harbour. I got askin' about a small 'aven where a sailor might rest quiet an' peaceful like an' fell in wi' a fisherman by the name of James Noble. It turned out I'd done a trip with his father in the old *ffaulcon* when I were a youngster. This Noble were an 'onest man an' told me about a small 'aven called Baytown just down the coast. It seemed just the sort of place I were lookin' for so I chartered 'im an' 'is boat to take me there.'

'My story is near over now as you may guess. Noble, he puts me ashore on Mill Beck Sands under High Scaur. "Not the Landing," he says, "it's right under their noses. Ask for a seaman called Bartholomew Storm. You can trust 'im. Tell 'im I do give you support. You will likely find 'im at this time in the Dock." Well, I did as I were told an' soon found Cap'n Storm. When I told 'im I were on the *Bartholomew* agin the Armada, 'e were very 'elpful. They'd seen three Spanish galleons pass up the coast in a stiff blow but no local ships 'ad give' chase. Old Storm, 'e wished 'e could 'ave 'ad a go at the Spanish but as you know, 'twas mainly west country vessels that were involved.'

'I must say a word about the character of the Yorkshire sailormen. They were 'mazin' 'onest. When Noble lands me on the beach I drops me bundle an' a bag o' pistoles breaks open on the sand. 'E 'elps me pick 'em up, every one. Then Cap'n Storm helps me to find a berth an' later to secure this cottage not wantin' any reward. Natural, I gave 'em one or two pieces. It served 'em well for there was precious little gold about on this coast in 1590. Come to think about it I don't see much about nowadays either!'

Dick and Michael listened, totally absorbed. Annie had laid aside her dowsing rod and was sitting with her head cocked sideways and a look of rapt concentration on her face. She was picking up whole sentences and the outline of the old man was becoming clearer as he continued.

'Now, this is the windlass about which my 'ole story is wrapped. I come ashore wi' money, lots of it, an' my needs being frugal, I didn't spend the tenth of it. It's still here. It's been 'ere for 'undreds of years waitin' for the right folk to take it on. I've tried before to get the attention of the people who 'ave lived 'ere but only succeeded in frightening the deadlights out o' them. What I want to do is to hand over the resposibility of my share in the Spanish vessels to you with the heavy charge that you will spend it in a wise and God-fearin' way an' not jus' 'ide it away as I did. Will you do this for me?'

The room fell silent. Dick looked at his shoes. Michael's mind was a whirl of questions. Annie took a deep breath.

'You mean you want us to uncover your cache, wherever it is and to put your money to good use.'

Andrew grunted and coughed.

'That is my wish and charge. That you take the money an' the bars an' convert it to current coin of the realm.

Then to spend it to good use in all conscience. Will you do this for me?'

High above the cluster of tumbled cottages and crowded steps a black sky slanted into an ebb-pulled, plunging tide. Even through the darkness, a mash of seething water tumbled about the scaurs and gleamed white in the deepening night. The gale seemed bent on continuing for ever.

Dick sighed heavily and thought that it was up to him to give a satisfactory reply.

'Thank you Andrew. Thank you for your story and thank you too for your commission which we accept.'

Andrew heaved an even larger sigh and raised both hands level with his face, palms outwards. Then, shaking them by way of emphasis he spoke earnestly.

'Take a bar of iron an' dig out these two stones 'ere in the chimbley. Inside you'll find a pawlin bag. In that, if it 'asn't fallen through by now, you'll find two bars of Spanish gold, one of silver an' two small pouches of pistoles. The pistoles used to be universal currency but they'll probably 'ave to be changed into your money. Oh, an' there be a couple of finger rings there too.'

He rose and pointed, tapping on the stones of the chimney breast.

'I don't think anyone else 'as found it. I've never been far from the place an' I'd 'ave noticed the commotion. Now, let's get on with it! Time is something that plays tricks, especial when you're dead!'

The room sprang alive with everyone starting to talk at the same time.

'Quick Dad, get a crowbar or something!'

'I'll mark the spot!' shouted Michael.

'Hold on there, I'll get a hammer and chisel.'

Within the minute heavy thuds reverberated through the cottage and chunks of mortar and stone chips were flying about the room. A white dust soon fell on everything and footprints became evident on the carpet.

'Whatever are you doing?'

Framed by the doorway to the stairs, Sylvia stood aghast before the spectacle of Dick wielding a large hammer and belting the chimney wall with demented fervour. At first nobody took any notice of her. Michael, Dick and Annie, and was that someone else there as well, seemed totally engrossed in demolishing the wall of her parlour.

'Stop!'

Dick paused, the hammer in mid flight. All eyes turned towards Sylvia now advancing across the room.

'Would someone please tell me what is going on?'

'We..er..we think that there is something hidden behind the wall here,' began Michael sheepishly.

It sounded rather lame and it was not good enough for Sylvia. She looked at each one of them in turn.

'Before anyone attempts to destroy my home, I'd welcome an explanation or at least some kind of excuse. And why, pray, at night when everyone has gone to bed?'

Dick turned.

'We didn't want to bother you with the possibilities before we were certain but we all have good reason to believe that there is a treasure hidden behind this wall.'

Sylvia just stood there. Either her family had taken leave of their senses or this out of character behaviour had some basis in fact.

'The damage is done now, you might as well carry on. But you jolly well make sure you put it all right again tomorrow.'

Sylvia looked at them again and shook her head. Dick and Annie and this Michael fellow all intent on some wild search. She turned around to look for the other chap but there was nobody else in the room. She must have been more flustered by being woken up than she realised. She sank into a dusty chair.

By now there was a considerable hole in the wall. It was quite large enough to get a hand inside. Michael volunteered. Stepping close to the jambs of the fireplace he hooked his arm into the cavity.

'Well? Is there anything there?'

Michael reached around in the blackness, soft with the cobwebs of centuries.

'I think there is. Yes, there's something here. It's all soft and flaky. It's a covering for something hard.'

'Let's have a look!'

'There's a smaller bundle here at the back.'

Michael stretched in further, his shoulder hard against the broken stonework. Slowly he extracted his arm to display a nest of greyish-black cobwebs surrounding a blacker pouch of cracked leather in his grasp. From the cracks in the bulging pouch there shone the gleam of dull gold.

Slowly, almost reverently, Michael lowered the pouch to the table and released his hold. Two pistoles of gold fell out and rolled across the dusty surface. In total silence, Michael stepped back for more until, true to the very word, there lay a blackened bar of silver, two larger bars of gold, so heavy that it took Michael and Dick another ten minutes to secure and a further bag of gold coins. The last to emerge were two large diamond finger rings set in gold and an unusual amber intaglio of a galleon set in silver.

'How on earth!' stared Sylvia.

'It's an almost unbelievable story,' answered Dick over his shoulder.

'Incredible!' added Michael.

'It's Andrew's legacy,' said Annie with some weight. 'It's our responsibility to see his wishes are respected.'

For the second time within the week Dick saw the image of Andrew slowly fade away. No-one else seemed to notice his departure. Fading too were the words that were the last he was to utter.

'God's will be done. Bargeist can come for me now! Farewell fellow shipmate. Fare ye well.'

Michael now took centre stage and the historian in him pressed to examine the artefacts before him on the table. He carefully looked at one of the coins and then at the bar of silver. He then turned out the other bag of coins.

'There's nothing here after 1582. These ingots are rough -cast for transport. Look, here is the foundry mark. It may still be possible to date the actual shipment from the Americas. At a first glance I'd say this was pre-Armada American gold bound for Spain just as we were told.'

There was no talk of sleep. They were all far too excited. Before dawn however, Sylvia had pieced together the whole story and had to accept that although incredible, the evidence lay before her on the table. Long before dawn problems had surfaced. How does one dispose of quantities of antique gold coins without alerting attention? Worse, how does one sell heavy gold bars without the certificates of purchase that inevitably went with them? Michael felt the best way was to declare 'treasure trove' and see the due process of law secure the pieces for national museums. Dick thought that that course would bring a great deal of publicity of the kind he'd rather do without. Annie was for filtering the coins into the collector's world and the bars into the scrap jewelry trade in Birmingham.

'You might not get as much for them, but it would be very discreet and no-one would ever know. I know of a goldsmith in Birmingham who buys large quantities of scrap gold for manufacturing jewelry. I'm sure he would buy from us with no questions asked.'

Now that Sylvia had learned the whole story and had seen the proof with her own eyes and even perhaps caught a glimpse of Andrew himself, she felt that Andrew's wishes should remain at the forefront of any decisions.

'He wanted the money to do some work, not go into a museum. Did he not remind you that it would need conversion into modern cash?'

'That's right,' said Michael. 'It goes against the grain, but that is what he said.'

'So let's decide. We keep quiet about this. If ever it surfaces or in the future one of us lets it out, we keep the location of this cottage a secret. There are hundreds of cottages in Bay and it would take a pretty good detective to discover which one held the treasure especially as repairs are being carried out all the time. We can fill the hole up before dawn and nobody will ever be the wiser. We trust the bars and the gold to Annie and her goldsmith friend and agree to take whatever is offered by the trade. Now, what do we do with the money?'

Dick went out into the kitchen where, under the sink, he kept a small bag of cement and a trowel. There was often a bit of pointing to be done after the winter. He mixed up a good dollop and returned to the parlour. While he was busy filling in the hole, the discussion ranged over many possibilities. There seemed to be a degree of concensus on the idea of using the money to support holidays for folk in need. Thinking of Sara's love and need for Bay, Michael thought this was a fine idea. Dick had learned that Bay had been a haven for Andrew and it was certainly a refuge for him. Sylvia thought that time out in Bay could only do a person good and Annie knew of several people who could never afford the luxury of a week or two away from the town and would never ask for it.

By dawn, the cottage was looking neat and tidy again, the treasure was ferried up-bank in three loads and locked in the boot of Dick's car. Dick would drive down to Annie in a week or so. Despite some reservations about the car, Dick knew that it would be the last place anyone would think of for a load of bullion.

As suddenly as it had begun and true to Andrew's words, the gale whispered out leaving only the sea to subside more slowly. By lunchtime the world was clean and fresh again. Only a solitary crab stranded at the bottom of Tyson's Steps told of the night's fury.

The following day Annie left Bay and returned by bus and train to her home. Michael promised to stay in touch. He had been much taken with this warm, intelligent woman whose knowledge of the paranatural or the supernormal surpassed his own. She had fully understood Sara, a barrier that most would baulk at. They had both followed the dowsing path, which, if given its head will lead the dowser into the area of greatest sensitivity. For them both it had been the delicate area of spirits in crisis.

Sylvia pondered long and thoughtfully on the whole issue. She'd found a quotation from 'The Family Reunion' by T S Eliot in the bookshop. It went like this:

"In an old house there is always listening, and
more is heard than is spoken.
And what is spoken remains in the room, waiting
for the future to hear it.
And whatever happens began in the past, and
presses hard on the future."

She thought it rather apt in the circumstances.

It was two months before Annie could report back on the results of their plan. The two gold bars had passed into the scrap gold trade in Birmingham at fourteen thousand pounds each. The silver had made two thousand. The pistoles went to a coin dealer where, surprisingly, they produced twelve thousand pounds mainly due to their condition. The rings were the best of all and went to a dealer in New York who had a collector in mind. The two diamond rings went for twenty four thousand pounds and the intaglio carving of the ship for three thousand, seven hundred and fifty pounds. The total, less various commissions and outlays, topped sixty five thousand pounds, quite sufficient for their project.

By the end of November, everything had miraculously fallen into place and all was ready. Dick found the continued excitement of it all quite exhilarating and couldn't stop grinning. It was going to be very hard for him not to tell everyone about it. Sylvia was a little more circumspect and kept a still tongue, avoiding any conversations that might lead to questions about her recent purchase. Annie, who had been involved with all the practical details, was extremely careful throughout the whole exercise and made doubly sure that the only other person to know names and destinations was Michael.

So the business of Andrew's legacy entered a fresh stage of development and it needed only the arrival of the first beneficiaries to see the plan in action. They all hoped sincerely that Andrew would approve.

When Sylvia came to share her T S Eliot with Dick she found that he too had discovered a quotation. It was from a book he'd taken out of the Whitby library. Called '*In search of Ghosts*' by Ian Wilson, it stated:

"..rather than ghosts seeming to offer the most tantalisingly intangible evidence for their own existence, we find that in reality they lie at the cutting edge of proof of the existence of life after death, and of our potential understanding of what life may be all about."

'There's no denying how far we've come in our understanding of these things,' said Dick.

'Or where it may lead us yet!' smiled Sylvia.

By five o clock on a still, late December evening all Bay's magic was contained within its darkly delineated twin headlands. The moon, a bruised orb of heavy gold, heaved itself higher and higher, its light hardening through the dancing sea-lace that lay glittering at its foot. All day long the colours had been leaching from the piled brown-stoned buildings so that the promised darkness lacked all definition save that of the drawn line in a silver wash. The air was glass but without the promised frost and the battering winds of the previous weeks had blown themselves out. Hours before a burnt orange solstice dawn would draw out above the ancient gabled bulk of Peak two people, a mother and her young daughter had settled happily into a cottage at Robin Hood's Bay. The lady was to leave well rested and her daughter Lucy vowed that she'd return one day.

As they travelled homewards Lucy turned to her mother and said, 'I really do believe in Father Christmas.' Her mother smiled and replied, 'Lots of children do dear.' 'No, I don't mean the pretend Father Christmas, I mean the real one. I saw him on Christmas Eve in the cottage. He came into my room. He was wearing a big cloak and looked so friendly and kind. He was singing too so I just knew it was him.'

Her mother smiled again. It was lovely to discover the magic of Christmas after so many difficult times. Perhaps they ought to come back in the summer now that she knew how.

Is it carols or shanties they sing at Christmas? Perhaps it's both.

15
93

POSTSCRIPT

The tune of the shanty that Andrew sang suggests that it was a variant of 'The *Verity* Pinnace', popular from early Elizabethan times. Contrary to the belief that sea shanties derived from the deep south of North America where they transferred to ships from the plantations, there is a considerable body of evidence to suggest that they were in common use on European vessels from the thirteenth century both for encouraging and supporting the working day and for entertainment.

'The *Verity* Pinnace' described the lives of various members of the crew in popular roles such as the vulnerable ship's boy, the bully Bosun, the martinet Captain or the lazy cook. Each section of five of six verses described one such role. The verses here are from the section descibing the fate of a ship's boy. Each verse is followed by the chorus, thus making the shanty adjustable to the length of a particular task.

The *Verity* Pinnace.

Little Peter shipped to sea
Aboard the pinnace *Verity.*
The Bosun soon he chased 'im round
Until the little bugger drowned.

Chorus

'Eave 'an 'aul,
Pawl by pawl,
Cattin' up the anchor!
'Eave 'an 'aul,
Large or small,
Mains'l or the spanker!

Cap'n then drew near to see,
Aboard the pinnace *Verity*,
Where little Peter's end were found
An' Bosun cruelly did 'im 'ound.

Chorus.

'Bosun, stand by me!' says he,
Aboard the pinnace *Verity*,
Then Cap'n, Mate and Master 'greed
To make the wicked bugger bleed.

Chorus.

The Bosun, he stepped up to flee,
Aboard the pinnace *Verity*,
But Cap'n were too quick for 'im
An' ran 'im through for 'is foul sin.

Chorus.

For those of 'ee who'd go to sea
Aboard the pinnace *Verity*,
Fear not that 'ee will 'arried be
The crew agree most pleasantly.

Chorus.

Tune by Stuart Tonnar.
Transcribed by Geoffrey Bunce